The Little French Recipe Book

JACKY DURAND

Translated from French by Sarah Robertson

HODDER

First published in France in 2019 by Editions Stock
An Hachette France company

First published in Great Britain in 2020 by Hodder & Stoughton
An Hachette UK company

This paperback edition published in 2020

1

A CIP catalogue record for this title is available from the British Library

Paperback ISBN 978 1 529 38239 6
eBook ISBN 978 1 529 38240 2

Typeset in Bembo MT Pro
by Palimpsest Book Production Ltd, Falkirk, Stirlingshire

Printed and bound in Great Britain by Clays Ltd, Elcograf S.p.A.

Hodder & Stoughton policy is to use papers that are natural, renewable
and recyclable products and made from wood grown in sustainable forests.
The logging and manufacturing processes are expected to conform
to the environmental regulations of the country of origin.

Hodder & Stoughton Ltd
Carmelite House
50 Victoria Embankment
London EC4Y 0DZ

www.hodder.co.uk

My life is nothing but a recipe unfolding, day by day, with its highs and lows.

Pierre Gagnaire, chef

PART ONE

I

I cannot drag my eyes away from your hands on the hospital bed cover. They are translucent, like tissue paper. They look like stranded roots on the bed of a stream. To think I once knew them when they were so warm and alive, despite being scorched from the palm to the flesh of the index finger. You'd say, laughing, that you were 'King of the Burns'. You might have kept a cloth wedged in your apron, but it was quickly forgotten when the bistro got busy. You'd grab those frying pans and even turn over veal chops or fillets of perch with your fingers. And you'd burn yourself without saying a word: one moment your hands were in boiling hot oil, the next turning out cakes from the oven.

You'd tell me that one burn got rid of another, a belief you owed to the old baker who taught you how to make bread as a child. You'd laugh when I touched your calloused scars. I also liked to play with the last joint of your index finger, as knotty as the foot of a vine, while asking you to tell me once again the story of how it came to be so deformed. You'd say that you were barely older than me at the time. You were sitting at the table where your mother had just put down her mincer to make a terrine. This cast-iron machine fascinated you. You were allowed to turn the handle while your mother fed it pieces of pork.

Except one day she left you alone and you put your index finger into the mincer. They had to run to find the doctor, who was on the main road, before returning with him in his cart. The doctor examined your finger. In those days it was unthinkable to ask a doctor any questions. He ordered your father to carve two splints from a piece of poplar wood. You gritted your teeth when he placed them over your finger and squeezed them tight with bands made from one of your father's flannel belts. He said he would come back to check it in a month.

When he removed the splint, your index finger was all pink and the last phalanx pointed to the left. The doctor said your finger had been saved but you might be turned down for military service. Your father frowned and declared that you'd do your service just like everyone else. You shook your head when you told me this, saying with a sigh: 'If only he'd known I'd do twenty months in Algeria.' And you carried on scraping the bottom of saucepans with the nail of that deformed finger, saying it was very useful for scouring the bits that were difficult to get to.

I remember your index finger poised on the back of a knife or a pastry bag. You'd apply yourself as if you were taking your professional pastry exam. Now, as I lift your finger from the bed cover, it seems so light and tiny to me, like a bone from a battery hen. I often wanted to bend that part of your finger to try and straighten it out, even though just the thought of doing it has always terrified me. No, I can't do that to you. Even when you die, I won't do it. It's because of a story we used to tell each other as kids at primary school, which has haunted me ever since. It was about an undertaker preparing a body. The father of a school friend had tried to straighten the leg of this dead woman, withered by cancer. The leg broke and the undertaker was fired.

I touch your hands once more, lightly. I want to see them

move, even just a millimetre. But they look like the spatulas you'd hang from the cooker hood after you'd made them dance in your hands, turning potato pancakes for a whole service. I search the bedside table for the aftershave I got you at Christmas. Pour un Homme by Caron. The shop assistant at the Gare de Lyon station in Paris had told me: 'You'll see, this one's good for a man of his age.' I shaved you the morning of 25 December. You stopped my hand:

'What's this?'

'A nice scent.'

'I've never used it.'

You allowed me to put a few drops on your neck before grumbling: 'A cook doesn't use scent. If they do, they ruin their nose and taste buds.' You sniffed it a bit, warily, before exclaiming, 'All these things you make me do!' I cover my hands in the cologne and gently massage your fingers and palms.

Three days ago, after I'd finished the dinner service, sleep was eluding me. I decided to drive around town in the van. I lit a Camel cigarette while listening to Led Zeppelin's 'No Quarter'. 'My noise', as you called it. The night was cold, the streets deserted. For a moment I hesitated, wondering whether to have a beer at the Café de la Paix. But I wanted to see you. I carried on to the hospital. I tapped in the code for the door of the palliative care ward that Florence, the night nurse, had given me. The hall was bathed in an orange half-light. The door to your room was ajar and, in the glow of the night light, I saw your hands creating a strange play of shadows, your eyes shut. You were rubbing your palms together as if you were kneading sweet pastry for the lemon tart on your dessert menu. Then you spread your fingers, pinching at them vigorously. Were you trying to remove little bits of pastry? I sat down by the side of the bed and watched you. I whispered in your ear: 'You're not losing your touch, Dad.' I wasn't expecting an answer. I just wanted you to hear me. I felt the calm footsteps of someone approaching from behind.

'What's he doing?' Florence asked softly.

'He's kneading. I thought he was making shortcrust pastry but it's bread. Now he's removing the dough stuck to his fingers.'

'They're beautiful, those movements.'

I glanced at her. 'How long until he goes?'

'He'll decide when.'

2

Tonight, I hear Florence's words once more. She watches over you, but it's Saturday, her day off. Before you sank into the coma three weeks ago, you'd discuss cooking a lot with her at night. You'd describe your dishes to her: poached eggs in *vin jaune* and chanterelle mushrooms, or vine peaches in syrup. You'd make her mouth water telling her how you made your quenelles. You'd shake your head when I said she was charming you in order to get your recipes. 'She won't, nor will anyone else,' you'd say over and over with a mischievous laugh.

Florence is genuinely fond of you. I get the feeling she finds your solitude touching. For the last six months that you've been in hospital, she's turned a blind eye to my comings and goings. 'This is inedible,' you declared when presented with your first hospital meal. And so I'd been delivering the 'little bites' you'd asked for. I'd carefully lay out a red checked tablecloth on your bed. I'd present you with dishes, depending on what you fancied: potato salad, celeriac remoulade, ham baked in hay, herring fillets and potatoes in oil, pâté en croûte. And always a bit of cheese: some twenty-three-month-old Comté, Époisses, or a Saint-Marcellin. You wanted an *île flottante*, just so you could tell me off for using 'too much vanilla'. I'd even stashed a small bottle of wine in my rucksack along with a wine glass. It had to be a red for you, with notes of spice and black fruit.

The night before you fell into the coma, I could only feed you little bits. An apple compote with a touch of cinnamon and lemon. You were no longer speaking. Since then, you've not eaten a thing. They feed you a cocktail of Midazolam and Skenan: one a sedative, the other morphine. You, who always said: 'If I find out one day I've had it, it'll be over quickly.' Who would have thought it would take you so long to die?

One evening I asked Florence: 'Why is he hanging on like this?' After a silence which seemed to stretch on forever, she replied: 'Maybe he's giving you time to say goodbye?' The answer left me feeling uncomfortable. It's haunted me ever since. Sometimes I feel guilty about your coma. I think that, what with my hand-wringing, my misery at being the one to live, I'm making you suffer and stopping you from going. One day I leant in to whisper in your ear, trying to say: 'Dad, go now if you want to', but the words wouldn't come.

As I lift your hospital gown to rub you with cologne, I uncover skin marbled with veins where your blood seems to be standing still. You'll go tonight. The certainty washed over me this morning as I began preparing the vol-au-vents for dinner this Valentine's day. Your regulars had asked me to make them, as you always serve them on 14 February. I began with the puff pastry. To start with, I divided it into two before rolling it out and using the pastry cutter to make circles for the base and rings for the top. Next, I assembled the vol-au-vents and brushed them with beaten egg. When they came out of the oven, I was disappointed with the result. My pastry had not risen enough. I didn't know you had to cook them for so long. I wished you were there to give me advice. I opened the window and lit a cigarette, sipping coffee in the freezing fog of the dark. It dawned on me then that you'd never be back in the kitchen, telling me off.

You never taught me a recipe. At least, not how they'd teach you at school. The absence of lists, quantities or lessons meant I had to use my eyes and ears to understand how you did things. When you said: 'Put some salt in', I would ask: 'Salt? Which salt? How much?' You'd roll your eyes, my questions irritating you. You'd grab my hand brusquely and put some coarse salt in it: 'You put it in the hollow of your hand, here, to figure out how much you need. Come on, it's not that difficult, you can measure anything using the palm of your hand.' When you spoke to me about 'a tablespoon of flour', I had to guess whether you meant a flat spoonful or a rounded spoonful. I could never get a cooking time out of you either. You'd say: 'You have a knife and a pair of eyes – that's more than enough to tell you if it's cooked or not.'

This morning, while cooking my crayfish in stock, I wondered once more where you had stashed away your recipe book. That book was a bit like a bubble that would float up to the surface of my memory. Sometimes it took just the smallest thing for it to surge forth as I daydreamed over a stove. The other day I was looking for an idea for stuffing a roast chicken when I remembered you'd sometimes put a Petit-Suisse cheese inside the bird. A memory comes back to me: it's a Sunday, you're lying in bed with Mum, both of you propped against your pillows. The recipe book is sitting on her thighs, she is chewing a pencil. I can sense you're annoyed by her questions as she teasingly taps your coffee cup: 'So, chef, when's your recipe for this chicken stuffing coming?' You roll your eyes. You hate being called 'chef'. You mutter into your coffee: 'You just stuff a Petit-Suisse up the chicken's arse.'

How many times have I remembered this scene when dithering

in front of my saucepan? How many times in my head have I flicked through your notebook while standing alone in my kitchen? I can see it now in Mum's hands, its leather cover, behind which flow your notes on ingredients, cooking times, tricks and flavours. As somebody who hates Béchamel sauce, I would have liked to learn it step by step, from words given form on a page, rather than having to spy constantly on your every move.

Instead of which, one day, in one of your icy fits of anger, you decided to make it disappear.

3

That afternoon I went to pick up Lucien so he didn't have to use his moped. Since you've been ill he has aged, and he is increasingly struggling in the kitchen. Now his back bends like a willow branch, whereas he used to stand so tall in front of your stoves. I never once heard you talk about him as your 'second'. You'd say 'Lulu' or 'my Lulu'. Lucien is a man of few words, but this afternoon in the minivan he asked me: 'How is he?' I could only reply, 'Stable.' I didn't have the heart to tell him you will die tonight. You mean everything to Lulu, and you know it.

He put on his apron and clogs. He kept a close eye on me as I assembled the vol-au-vents. He saw the truffle I wanted to grate over the dish just before serving it. I asked him why he was smiling. He replied: 'Do you remember the old man's face when you added truffle to his pâté en croûte? When he said that it was "no longer his recipe and you obviously had money to waste"?'

It's true, I realise, I never saw you cook with truffle. You'd say, 'Not local, too expensive. Besides, it overpowers a dish's other flavours.' You've only ever sworn by the girolle mushrooms that grow near Lulu's house, which he'd bring to you by the basketful.

One day I actually thought I'd found it, your damn recipe book. Lulu was napping in the back courtyard; you'd gone to pick cherries for the *clafoutis*. I rummaged through the bags hanging off Lulu's moped and found the edge of a leather cover among the dirty rags. I was about to take it out of the bag when Lulu caught me. 'What are you looking for, kid?' he asked in a voice devoid of all anger. I felt my face go red. I couldn't imagine lying to Lulu. He was too open, too humble. I quietly said: 'I thought I could see Dad's recipe book.' Lulu told me to empty the contents of the bags. The leather turned out to be an old exercise book cover containing carefully folded pages of newspaper: 'I use them to wrap the fish when I go fishing. And vegetables and mushrooms too,' he explained as I stood there weakly. I didn't know how to explain to Lucien that – ever since he'd tried to burn it in the coal stove – all I could think about was my father's recipe book. As he closed the bag, Lucien said to me softly: 'Don't think about it any more, otherwise the old man will kick off.'

Lucien has called you the 'old man' ever since you were all of twenty and were his sergeant in Algeria. You never once had to give him an order in your kitchen. You always said to me that Lulu could read your mind when you were studying the cliffs in search of a cave where Fellaghas might be hiding. In the kitchen, too, he could always tell when you didn't like a sauce, and he always had a bit of butter and flour to hand to bring it back.

Tonight I left him to it to prepare the cheese gougères for the aperitif. I couldn't face telling him I needed the whole space to do the vol-au-vents. Lucien also likes fussing over Guillaume, the apprentice, to whom he has taught his recipe. He is surprisingly talkative with the boy and has showed him how to shape the gougères with a soup spoon. I hate to admit it, but I never knew *you* to be so patient. We had a quick snack before the service.

Lucien and Guillaume picked at the meat on the chicken carcass whilst I nibbled on a gougère. I really fancied a good wine. When I went down to the cellar and brought up a bottle you'd given me as a present, a Beaune wine called Le Clos l'Enfant Jésus, Lucien stared at me for the longest time with his Buster Keaton eyes. I went to get three beautiful long-stemmed wine glasses. 'Drink', I said to Guillaume, 'it's a good one.'

I wish you could have seen Lucien and me assembling the vol-au-vents. Guillaume had prepared some very hot plates. We arranged the meat in the middle of the puff pastry, adding the small quenelle scoops, the sauce dripping around the sides of the case. I grated some truffle over the top. Chloé, the young woman who did a little extra waitressing for us, couldn't take the plates from the serving hatch. I asked her if she was worried about handling hot dishes. She said no, it was just that my vol-au-vents were so beautiful, she'd never seen anything like them. In the restaurants she had worked in they used mass-produced puff pastry and filling that came from a tin. Your words came back to me: 'We make everything here, otherwise you can't call it cooking.'

At 9.30 p.m. I left Lucien, Guillaume and Chloé to finish up service. I slowly made my way up to the hospital. You could cut the fog with a knife tonight. I sat down on a park bench to smoke a cigarette. I thought back to when I would take you for a walk in your wheelchair, the leaves glowing golden in the October light. You had told me off for lighting a cigarette: 'Don't do that – look where it's got me.' I asked you why you had chain-smoked unfiltered Gitanes cigarettes all your life, from your first coffee in the kitchen till ten at night, when you polished the stainless steel of your hob. You muttered: 'It helped me to keep going.' I knew I couldn't ask you any more about it.

As I came into your room I knew this would be our last night together. After finishing with the cologne on your skin, I tried to arrange what was left of your hair, since the radiotherapy had burnt most of it off. I knew you had agreed to this last round of treatment for me, hoping to snatch a handful of weeks from death. Still, I blame myself for making you endure all those horrendous rays down in the hospital basement. I touch your mouth; it looks like the crust of dry bread. The other day it was like a hideous crater gurgling fetid water. I got the impression that your lungs were filling, about to drown you. I called the nurse, who just shrugged her shoulders. I moisten your lips with a bit of the Clos l'Enfant Jésus. I pour a little into the glass on your bedside table for myself and say, 'To you, Dad', drinking it in one go. The wine burns in the pit of my stomach, a sensation that seems to grow as your breathing diminishes. I remember the first drop of wine I ever tasted with you. I must have been ten years old. We had gone to Corgoloin on a grey Sunday morning in January. You used to be a regular visitor of a winegrower there, who rolled his 'r's in a gravelly voice. Standing at the foot of every barrel, you'd taste the wine. The winegrower would talk a lot; you'd just say a few words after having rolled the wine around your tongue. We were sitting on a wooden block; you'd brought some very hard little goat's cheeses and hunks of your bread. I instantly loved the sharp taste of the Pinot Noir with the cheese.

The clock on the wall of your room says 10.30. I take off my shoes and my old brown zip-necked sweater. I sit on the edge of the bed and take you in my arms. I tell you: 'You know you could have heard a pin drop when they were eating the vol-au-vents earlier. It was just the sound of the knives and forks on the plates, scraped clean by the end. And you're right about the truffle, it's always too much, except maybe in an omelette. My cooking would never had made any sense, nor had any flavour without you. You taught me without saying a word. You can go now, Dad. We've had a good life together, even though some days it didn't seem like it. I love you and will always love you. Just like I love and will always love Mum.'

Your chest collapses into a long final breath, like a birthday balloon deflating. I kiss you and pull the sheet up around your neck. I close the door, whispering to the nurse, 'He's gone.'

Outside, the icy fog chills me to the bone. I wonder how you'll be in the frozen earth. Lucien is waiting for me in the kitchen; he is reading a newspaper on the counter. I say again, 'He's gone,' and fill up two glasses with the rest of the wine. Without thinking I open the table drawer, as if I'm going to find the recipe book. All I find is a packet of tissues. It seems you've taken it to your grave. That empty drawer; it's as if you've just died a second time.

4

It's a Sunday morning in winter, I must be five years old. The sunny day is piercing through the shutters. You've tried tiptoeing downstairs, but the wooden stairs still creak with every step as you descend to your kitchen. You light the coal kitchen stove, your large cooking pot with handles banging the sides of the sink as you fill it. You always insist on hot water when you're at your stove. You've been told again and again that you've got the hot-water boiler to do that for you, but no, you've got to have water bubbling away on the cooker. 'Bubbling but not boiling,' you say. 'Water destroys everything at a hundred degrees.' The roar of your coffee grinder comes next. You hate the percolator-made espresso served in the restaurant. You need your 'army juice', as you call it. A mix of arabica and robusta to create your favourite sharp, smoky-flavoured coffee. You make enough for a whole regiment in that large metal cafetière of yours. You keep it warm on the edge of the stove until your last cup, before you go up to bed. Only you can drink this coffee, 'strong enough to wake the dead', as Lucien says while he brews his tea.

When the smell of coffee wafts upstairs, I get up. I scamper into your room because I want to check if Mum is still sleeping. What I really dread is to find an empty bed, that she's gone. It's a strange fear that always grips my chest. And yet just yesterday she said, 'I love you' as I lay in my bed, clinging to her. I always have to hold her tight before falling asleep. At night Mum smells of the Nivea cream that she applies to my cheeks, which are chapped by the cold. As for you, every night you shout out 'Night, night, kid' from your bedroom. And last night, you added: 'Are you going to make brioche with me tomorrow?' I shouted a big 'YES', laughing merrily. Mum whispered to me: 'And let me sleep in tomorrow, you little rascal.' This morning I gently push open the door to see her dark brown hair poking out between the duvet and the pillow where her head is buried. Dad is whistling in his kitchen.

I'm still holding my cuddly toy – an old teddy bear with tatty fur – as I join you at the stove. 'You're already up,' you say, feigning surprise as always. 'Don't put your teddy near the stove. You've already burnt one of his ears. Are you hungry?' I shake my head no. You pick me up by the waist and set me down on your worktop. The stainless-steel surface freezes my buttocks through my pyjamas. Having plunged a ladle into your pot of boiling water, you start to moisten the coffee. I like the nonchalant concentration of this act. You take out some coffee before the cafetière is quite filled, then come and sit beside me. You put your nose into your mug, blowing and inhaling it at the same time. You feel for your packet of Gitanes in your pocket. You take one out and tap it on the stainless-steel surface. You flick your lighter by rubbing it on your thigh, then inhale the smoke deeply into your lungs. It's just one of things, but all it takes is the warm feel of your skin to make me love the musky smell of tobacco.

You stub out your cigarette and, with a clap of your hands, command: 'Let's tackle the brioche!' You take out a cube of yeast from the larder. I'm allowed to crumble it into the milk you've poured into a bowl. I smell the mix; the aroma intoxicates me. It smells like Mum, quite sharp, but sweet when it's heated. You pour in flour gradually alongside the eggs. Same with the salt, you don't weigh a thing but juggle one spoon for measuring and one for tasting. They're always kept close to hand. When it's all go in the restaurant, and you've dipped them in some veal jus or rhubarb compote, you rinse them in a pitcher of water then wipe them vigorously with your tea towel. You ignore the chef's white hat and uniform. It's always a blue apron over a white T-shirt and jeans for you, your bare feet in big black leather clogs. Sometimes, waiting between dishes, you tap your spoon on the cooker guardrail to the rhythm of the Sardou or Brassens song you're humming. On Sundays you listen to cassette tapes in the kitchen. Particularly Graeme Allwright. You know all the lyrics of 'Waist Deep in the Big Muddy' by heart. Your eyes widen as you roar: 'We were in water up to our necks and the old fool told us to keep going', then adding to me: 'Now make me a pile of flour like sand.' With delight I plunge my hands into the flour, which feels like silk between my fingers. I push my hands across the stainless steel, pressing down on the white powder, revelling in its touch. I also love the salt crust of a prime rib of beef; the skin of an onion crinkling between my fingers; the woodiness of a cinnamon stick or the velvety skin of a ripe August peach.

'Now make a tunnel in the middle of the flour.' Your hands gently guide mine until it's time for you to pour in the milk and yeast. I want to break the eggs. 'Hang on, we'll do it a different way.' You place a bowl in front of me. I must break the egg on the side of the bowl, but I make a real hash of it and manage to mix yolk and egg white with the shell. You smile: 'Not to worry.' You take another egg and bowl but you don't throw away a thing: not the outer skin of a leek, the carcass of a chicken or the skin of an orange. You possess the art of transforming all of these into a stock or powder. 'If he could, your father would recycle the smoke of his Gitanes cigarette,' Lucien says of you. 'Start again' is what you say to me, as you remove the shell from my previously broken egg. I am elated when I manage to break the second one properly. You beat the eggs vigorously before blending them into the flour. You stand behind me. I feel your firm grip over mine: 'Right, now we have to knead and knead.' I apply myself seriously to begin with, but soon start to laugh when my fingers get stuck to the mix. You scold me: 'Don't mess around, you need to make the dough elastic.'

You add some softened butter. I lick my fingers. I like the taste of the little knobs of butter you fetch every Sunday from the cheesemonger, along with your cream and cheese: Comté, Morbier and Bleu de Gex. You say to me, 'That's good', placing the dough in a basin and covering it with a cloth. 'Just wait and see how it doubles in size. Right, come on, let's go and get Mum's oysters now.'

We live in a little town where the sea is a distant dream. In the lane leading up to the Place de la Mairie, a strange cavern seems to be carved into the rock. This is the fishmonger's and, for my five-year-old self, an anxiety-inducing lair. The boss has a face like one of his John Dory fish. He sniffles constantly, seems always to have a cold, whether it's summer or winter. He makes noises that sound like he's grunting, his mouth full of pebbles as he sips his white wine, which he serves with fistfuls of grey prawns. I press my face against the glass of the fish tank. The dance of the trout mesmerises me, filling me with sadness. I lament their coming death, the blow of a wooden club on their heads. I'm sad in the same way when I catch Mum alone in the bed you share, looking out of the window.

The other day she was naked in a mass of undone sheets. She didn't see me come in. She was smoking one of Dad's Gitanes. She seemed far away in a cloud of cigarette smoke. I can usually tell when she's lost in the world of one of her books, but this time she seemed to be somewhere where neither I nor Dad belonged. I was grateful when she turned with a start as I crunched on my sweet. She pulled the sheets up to her shoulders and smiled at me.

5

When you come back, you put your bag of oysters on the windowsill. 'Have you seen the dough? It's doubled in size.' With my index finger I touch it, this bloated belly which gives off a wonderful smell of yeast. I don't understand why you have to mistreat it, as you knock it back then fold it over. 'You'll see, it's going to get even bigger,' you promise. You unfold your paper, the *Est Républicain*, over the steel counter, before lighting a cigarette. You lean over its pages, left hand and right elbow on the worktop. I've always known you like this, reading your newspaper in the morning. I know I mustn't disturb you. It's not so much the content of the newspaper but the act of reading it that's important to you. You decode words in the same way you taste your cooking: meticulously, never fully satisfied. You started too young in the kitchen to be confident of your knowledge. While you know the rules of grammar and conjugations, your pen hovers uncertainly over the paper when you have to write out a purchase order. Yours is the joyful curiosity of someone self-taught when you learn a new word or discover some other world on television as I sit on your knees. You like the *Five Columns on the Front Page* show that deals with current affairs, and Frédéric Rossif's nature programmes. Yet you seem ashamed when you watch Mum marking her students' schoolwork. One day you opened one of her literature anthologies, then briskly shut it again, as if you'd been caught red-handed. Mum smiled and said gently: 'The book wasn't going to eat you.' Much later, you told me about whole villages in Algeria where no one could read or write.

Mum is a literature teacher at school. You tell her she's your 'posh little clever-clogs' all the time, which winds her up. You didn't speak to her like that when you first laid eyes on her. It was a September day of rain and wet leaves. She opened the door, eyes stinging from the cigarette smoke. Nicole hadn't noticed her as she prepared a round of Picon beers. It was Lucien who tugged the sleeve of her blouse as he came up from the cellar. Nicole got annoyed. He had disturbed her while she was getting the 'workman's lunch' menu ready. 'Would you like to eat?' 'Do you need cutlery?' Mum shrugged her shoulders, intimidated. Nicole surveyed a room of regulars at their tables. At your restaurant everyone had their place, practically their own napkin ring. You couldn't just seat a stranger anywhere. Nicole hesitated for a moment then asked her: 'If I clear the little table by the window, would that be all right?' Mum said yes, smiling shyly. Nicole removed the succulent plants and old magazines from the table, unfolded a paper tablecloth and laid a plate and some cutlery over it. Mum sat down, not daring to say the three-course set menu would be a bit much for her. Although actually, while she didn't touch the jug of wine, she ended up polishing off the whole meal. It was beetroot and lamb's lettuce salad, followed by a roast with boulangère potatoes and apple tart to finish.

She came back the next day and on the days that followed, always sitting in the same place, a book by her plate. Nicole was utterly intrigued by how someone could eat and read at the same time. Some of the clientele went as far as offering her an aperitif

or a coffee, but she always declined politely with a quick smile.
One day you poked your head through the serving hatch to take
a look at this unusual, solitary diner. You smiled. Nothing more.
The first time you two spoke was on a Friday. You were cooking
hake with sautéed potatoes cut into squares, prepared over a high
heat in your copper-bottomed Val-d'Ajol sauté pan. You were
vigorously shaking them when Nicole shouted out to you: 'The
young lady sitting alone has asked if she can have an extra serving
of the potatoes.' You piled up a huge plate of them, added a
sprinkle of chives, and took them over to her yourself. My mother
saw your deformed finger and your blue eyes first. You said,
'Henri, at your service.'

She laughed. 'There's three times more than I can eat there.'
You shrugged your shoulders and gently mocking, said, 'Miss?'
'Hélène.'
'At my place, Miss Hélène, we like things a lot or not at all.'
Apparently these were the words with which you seduced
Mum.

I watch as you place the brioche into the gaping black mouth
of your oven. It's the same when you open its door to baste
chickens with your all-purpose spoon. For me you are the master
of the fire, a magician when you make the brioche rise; an expert
safe-breaker when you prise open oysters and a wise king when
you whisk Chantilly cream and melt dark chocolate for me. The
smell of golden brioche and freshly squeezed orange juice perme-
ates the kitchen. It's the season for blood oranges. You peel their
skins then let me put the segments on a plate. You add a few
drops of orange-flower water. You say it reminds you of Algeria.

I take up a glass of orange juice for Mum. She has opened
the curtains, plumped up the pillows and is reading a thick book
through her tortoiseshell glasses. Mum reads all the time. On her

bedside table there are piles of books and magazines next to a pot of pencils. Sometimes she annotates books. It fascinates me that you can write on a printed page like that. 'Do you want to drink orange juice with me?' she asks. I say no. I am holding out for the brioche with Chantilly and chocolate.

You try to catch Mum's eye when she turns back to her book, nibbling on a bit of brioche. You stroke the cover of her large book. You feign innocence and ask: 'Who is Simone de Beauvoir then?'

'She's an author.'

'Ah, an author, is she?'

'You do get female authors, you know. Just like you can get female chefs.'

You burst out laughing and try to provoke her: 'That'll be the day! I'd like to see one of them bring up the coal from the basement to get a stove going.'

'You do know electric and gas cookers exist, don't you?'

'There's nothing like coal for keeping a pot simmering. Try taking my Lulu's coal away, it would kill him,' you say, removing Mum's tortoiseshell glasses from her nose.

'What are you doing?'

'What do you think I'm doing?'

Mum puts her glasses back on and glares at you. You try again, putting your arm around her. But she shakes her head for you to remove it.

You smile gently, embarrassed: 'It's Sunday.'

'So what?' Mum replies sharply.

I don't like the way she says, 'So what?' She turns a page and starts reading again. You get up, sighing gently: 'So nothing.'

You go back to your kitchen.

Alone with Mum in the room, I too feel like she doesn't want me there.

6

It wasn't so long ago that when you took off Mum's glasses and brought your face up close to her lips, she'd playfully turn her mouth away from you. She'd leaving you waiting, teasing you. 'Hmm, I think I quite fancy a cigarette, don't you?' You'd grab your packet of Gitanes from the bedside table, turn towards me and say, 'Go and play in your room, little lad.' I'd do what you told me, like a brave soldier, as you closed the door on me.

It wasn't so long ago that we were happy. Each summer you and Lulu would make a giant paella over a fire out the back of the restaurant. It was a sight to behold, with a mountain of rice, mussels, squid, chorizo, rabbit and chicken, all simmering on a fire skilfully maintained by Lucien. I was allowed to put a few twigs on the red-hot coals. Hanging up in the kitchen there used to be a picture of me, age three, sitting in the paella pan, with you and Lulu on either side holding my hands. Mum didn't like these kinds of jokes. She screamed at you the day you got her to come into the kitchen and lifted the lid of your big pot to show her where you'd been hiding me.

Every Sunday Mum asked you to get a large serving tray, but you stubbornly insisted on putting your paella pan on the bed instead. You'd joke that it was our *Déjeuner sur l'herbe*, like the

Manet painting, as you laid out the oysters, orange salad and warm brioche. We were never allowed to help ourselves, you had to prepare our plates for us. Oysters laid out in the shape of a star with buttered brown bread for Mum, and a large slice of brioche coated in warm chocolate and Chantilly for me.

Every Sunday you'd play out the same routine. You'd make a face like you'd forgotten something and rush back downstairs. Mum would wink at me as she popped a juicy oyster in her mouth. Waiting, I'd pick at my dome of Chantilly. We'd hear you coming up the stairs, slowly this time, savouring every step. You'd appear with a blue vase with three flowers and a flute of champagne in your right hand. Mum would smile, even as she shook her head. You would whisper to her 'for my princess' and sometimes you'd add, quietly, 'for my posh little slapper'. Mum would frown: 'Shut up.'

To this day, I can still see you two having your *Déjeuner sur l'herbe* on a Sunday. Mum is sitting cross-legged on the bed, sipping champagne between oysters. You have kept your apron on, your mug of coffee balanced on your knees and a pillow tucked behind your back. You chew on a segment of orange then light a cigarette. I don't think I've ever seen you sit down to eat your meals. Then again, could you really call it a meal when it was a case of you mopping up the last bit of a *bourguignon* straight from the pan with some bread, or scraping off whatever was left on the rind of a Comté with your knife? In summer you'd munch on a tomato with a pinch of salt; in winter you'd pull apart an endive and dip its leaves in vinaigrette. Sometimes, after a service, Lucien would make you both an omelette with the remains of a bunch of parsley, then you'd share a last slice of tart together. Apparently in Algeria you'd both do the same thing, eating barley bread dipped in olive oil and almonds rather than the regiment grub and combat rations. When Mum would tell you that you didn't eat properly, you'd say to her that you'd 'always been used to eating on the go'. It was what cooks did. You enjoyed cooking for others, not for yourself.

It took me some time to realise you did everything so that Mum never got close to a pan. Truth be told, in the little flat above the restaurant, we didn't even have a kitchen. Your stove was your kingdom, where Mum had no place. Rarely did she venture in, and she looked completely lost if she poked around for some sugar or a bit of compote to give me. The rest of the time our meals were placed in the serving hatch and we'd sit at the little table near the window, the one Mum had made her own. We would never have the set menu for the day. You made it your duty to always prepare 'something special' for us. Mum adored eating kidneys and you cooked them to perfection, just pink as she liked them, deglazed in port and bound with a base of veal, cream and mustard. For me you'd coat a slender escalope in crisp breadcrumbs. You'd worry and ask: 'Any good?' Mum and I would nod yes, our mouths stuffed like two little kids. But deep down, I knew you'd not given her permission to cook.

At our last *Déjeuner sur l'herbe*, Mum got you a present. Perhaps that bloody present marked the moment after which nothing would ever be the same again. She got out a thick notebook and placed it in front of you. Bound in beautiful natural leather, its pages ivory and soft to the touch, it had a red ribbon for a bookmark. You were intrigued:

'Is it for your work?'

Mum looked at you with that slightly weary tenderness she had when faced with your incomprehension. 'It's for writing down your recipes.'

'Writing down?' You repeated this several times, your voice

slowly getting louder. As far as you were concerned, it was as if she hadn't understood a damn thing about your work. Yes, you had become a cook. The Relais Fleuri ticked over, you kept the punters happy. You could have expanded, started doing banquets, weddings, and so on, but it was not about that, nor what your godawful life had been about; what had led you to a split-second choice between two trains. You'd been a baker's boy and a sergeant before, but deep down you knew nothing was set in stone, that it was down to destiny, or *mèktoub* as they said over on the other side of the Mediterranean. When you joined in the bar chatter, you often said: 'We've all got to have grub.' You'd become a cook in order to earn a crust. But who knows? Maybe you'd have liked to have become a merchant seaman, a doctor, or a water and forestry engineer. One day you stood up for a lad from a priority social housing estate who'd become an armed robber. The newspaper was covering his court case. As far as you were concerned, he'd become a robber 'because he wasn't from the middle-class part of town, he was from the wrong side of the tracks'. You said something that silenced the chatter in the bar:

'If I had to choose between two equally stupid things, give me a robber over a rich kid any day.'

'You can't say that, Henri,' a client had whispered.

'And why can't I say that then?' you'd replied, your voice cold. In films you always liked the bastards, the Samurais and the deserters over the heart-throb heroes.

I remember the day I introduced you to De Niro in *Taxi Driver*. You said to me: 'That could've been me if I hadn't come back from Algeria with Lulu.'

No one understood that resigned rage when you said: 'You've got to earn a crust.' Not even my mother. She had an *aggrégation* – the highest teaching diploma in France – and had restarted

28

work on her thesis on the eighteenth-century author 'Crébillon fils'. And now this recipe book? Why not throw in a Michelin star to boot? And, even worse, Mum said she would write down your recipes as you dictated them to her. 'And you'll write it like I talk, will you?'

She put her arms round your neck. 'You're crazy!'

'No, I'm in love with you.'

At first you played along with it. One Sunday afternoon, after you had sent me to play in my room, I came back to join you on the unmade bed. Mum was writing down your recipe for *poulet de Bresse*. She was using a pencil with a rubber attached so she could rub out the words when you wavered:

'You have to frizzle the chicken pieces in a large frying pan.'

'Frizzle?' Mum asked.

'You know, brown them!' you exclaimed, with a touch of contempt that seemed to say: 'She's a professor of letters and she doesn't even know what *frizzle* means?' You had laughed and I was relieved. Maybe this recipe book was a good idea after all.

Yet with each session of dictation you argued more and more. Mum was writing it as if it were a real book, and books terrified you, particularly cookbooks. They distanced you from Mum. You did not recognise yourself in her complicated words. When the recipes were written down, all their intuition, their taste, seemed to you to disappear. You suspected Mum was trying to take you away from your stove and elevate you into a social milieu that was not your own. You were confused; you felt as if she had offered you the notebook so that you could enter her world, a world of reading and writing. In the kitchen, when you were on your own from early in the morning till late at night, you convinced yourself more and more that Mum no longer loved you.

7

It's a Saturday, our day for brawn. I want to make it with you and Lucien. This morning, Lulu has arrived earlier than usual because you have to go and get a pig's head from the tripe seller. I have heard Lulu arriving on his pale blue moped. He drives *la bleue* — as he calls it – to work every day, twenty kilometres in the morning and twenty kilometres back, often in the pitch black, rain or shine. When it's parked in the back courtyard, I'm allowed to rummage through its leather saddlebags. In the right-hand bag, there's a kitchen rag covered in bike grease, a monkey wrench, a screwdriver and a bike pump that I play with. The left one has a jute bag that Lulu fills with mushrooms according to the season: mousserons, girolles and black chanterelles.

In the stories you tell, you and Lucien came back from Algeria together. After the boat transported you to Marseille, you both made your way up the hill to the train station, the Gare Saint-Charles, where Lucien checked the times for his train and asked you where you were planning to go. You had replied: 'Anywhere, as long as the main square has got a bakery and there's a place to sleep nearby.'

Lulu had suggested you should come with him. Although you knew his region well, you had never spoken to him about it.

You two had to change trains in a small town in eastern France. It was hot; you suggested having a beer while you waited. You came out of the station and saw a café-restaurant with a terrace overrun with geraniums. You sat down at a table. You ordered two halves from a seemingly ageless woman, whose legs were giving her trouble. That's when you saw the 'For Sale' sign. You sipped your beer slowly. Then, as you handed over your money to pay, you asked the woman, 'Are you the owner?'

She confirmed the fact.

'How much do you want for it?'

'You'll have to negotiate that with my husband. He's due back from hospital on Monday.'

You turned to Lulu: 'You up for it?'

He replied yes, although he added: 'You know I've never even picked up a pan.'

You replied, 'That's fine, you didn't know how to use a rifle once.'

Before taking the railcar you both turned to look at the bistro's façade. You said, 'We'll call it the Relais Fleuri. Is that OK with you?'

Lulu had said, 'It's always OK with you.'

The following Monday the deal was done.

To you brawn is more than just a recipe. It's how you approach cooking, starting with very little: a stale crust of bread, the remains of some meat. You cook dishes that would be inconceivable today, like breaded cow's udder. When we set off for the tripe seller at the covered market, the pig's head looms like a terrifying mythical creature to me. Lulu frightens me by saying that pigs can eat children, that gangsters use them to dispose of their enemies. The tripe seller laughs and winks: 'Are you buying my whole shop today then?' He offers me a piece of cervelat sausage, his fingers smelling of blood. As always, I feel for your hand when I'm nervous. You, however, are far too busy to pay any attention to me, delighted by his stall. You need a metre of beef skirt for your Saturday steaks, the only dish you do that day. Seeing your clients dip their chips in your magical gravy says it all. A spoon is perfect for scraping the last of the meat juice from the bottom of the frying pan. I dip dry bread into it.

You want it all: calf's feet to make the brawn jelly, pig's feet that you'll serve with vinaigrette and slices of white onion; veal kidneys, of course; andouillette sausages with a gratin, but also beef tongue done with a tomato sauce and gherkins. You turn to Lulu: 'What about a little salad of *gras-double* tripe for the menu? Lulu nods in approval. Lulu always says yes. The tripe seller gathers your packages together and asks: 'Anything else?' Though you've resigned yourself to stopping there, the tripe seller carefully cuts a thick slice of calf's liver with the flat of his knife. 'Here, this is for your lunch,' he says, adding in a bag of pork rind. I love pork rind.

I feel like I am in a war film when I watch you making brawn with Lulu. You two are so organised together, it's like the night before a battle. You have honed your knives with a sharpening steel, Lucien has gone into the pantry to find what he needs to make a good stock: carrots, onions, shallots and a sprig of parsley. He peels the vegetables while you carefully wash the pig's head in cold water. Your movements have a touch of reverence about them. One day I asked you: 'Are you frightened of hurting it?' You seemed surprised. You remained silent for a bit then you smiled gently at me: 'Respect for animals is important, living or dead. Even more so when you cook them.' As a teenager, your words came back to me when I learnt that – in his village – Lucien cleaned and prepared the bodies of the deceased before they went in the coffin. I didn't dare ask him about it, but I did ask you what on earth would make a man end up washing the dead. It was on one of the days you were in a bad mood. You said, grouchily: 'Lucien has never been frightened of the grim reaper or what he leaves behind.' A few weeks ago, when we were coming back from hospital, Lucien had said to me in the car: 'You know, we saw some things over there in Algeria.'

Lucien hoists me over the stove so I can see the pig's head in the huge cauldron. He adds onion studded with cloves, two calf hooves, thyme, bay leaf, pepper, nutmeg and some rough salt. You uncork a bottle of wine and pour it into the pot. It's the white that Lucien makes. He has a few rows of Chardonnay but also Noah, a grape that's been banned since the 1930s. The Noah grape is one of the secrets of *la pôchouse*, the fish stew you make for just a lucky few. People come from as far afield as Lyon, Strasbourg and even Paris to taste your ragout of freshwater fish. As soon as the fish season begins, Lucien gets on *la bleue* and sets off, bringing you back a constant supply of pike, perch, eels and tench. Sometimes the fish is still wriggling in his saddlebags when he returns to the restaurant. He will open his bag and stroke the fins and gills of a fish nestled amongst weeds. Not without pride, he will pull out a pike – the length of his arm – from the other saddlebag and you say, 'That is one hell of a gob. We'll do it with a beurre blanc sauce.' I rub garlic on the toasted slices of bread that accompany the *pôchouse*.

You sip a glass of Chardonnay with Lulu. The brawn simmers in the pan. From time to time you use the ladle to remove the impurities that bubble up to the surface of the stock. You peel the Bintje potatoes for your chips. You frown: 'Go ask your mum if she's eating here for lunch.' I don't like it when you talk about

Mum this way. These days she's like a stranger in the house and you don't know how to talk to her any more.

Mum barely ever eats in the restaurant now.

At lunch I eat in the school canteen while she lunches with her colleagues. At night you leave a tray of food on the staircase. We eat dinner together in front of the television. You two just cross paths occasionally: you're in the kitchen from seven in the morning till eleven at night. You only speak to each other if it's about my work at school, why my fingers are forever stuffed in my mouth, and the exercise books I struggle to write in.

Through the wall separating our rooms I listen to you talk, you and Mum. It's never shouts or tears, just monotone voices and resigned silences. You often get up in the dark. Your bare feet make the floorboards creak. You gently close the bedroom door behind you and put on your noisy clogs. I have this memory: one night when I have toothache, I can hear you on the staircase. I decide to come down as well so you can look after me. I tiptoe into the kitchen. I find you asleep, fully dressed. You're on the camp bed that Lucien uses to nap on between services or when the weather is so bad that he can't drive home on his moped. You're hunched up in a ball and I'm scared to wake you. I climb up on a stool to reach the spice rack. I'm about to open a jar when you wake up and whisper, 'What on earth are you doing?'

I moan, 'I wanted you to put a clove on my tooth because you said it's good for when it hurts.'

You look so sorry. You lift me off the stool and put me down on the ground. You tell me to open my mouth and you say, 'Which one is bothering you?'

I show you a molar. You put a clove on it. 'Do you want some hot milk?'

I snuggle up to you while you put a pot on the still-warm stove. You light a Gitane and turn up the radio very gently. Mort Shuman is singing 'Le Lac Majeur'. It seems to me that I've always lived like this with you. I ask you if I can stay up all night too.

'No,' you say, smiling.

'How come you can, then?'

'Because I'll always be a baker, even if I'm a cook now. When I learnt to make bread, I used to have to start work at two in the morning.'

I know there's some truth in what you're telling me. The truth of your younger self that is only ever alluded to in fragments. But talking about your past life as a baker also serves to draw a veil over your existence now. You don't make bread at night any more and you don't share a bed with Mum either. I finish my milk.

'You have to go back up to bed now,' you tell me. I put my arms around your neck.

'What about you?' I ask.

'I'm going to stay here and get ahead with my desserts,' you reply.

I cross Mum on the stairs. She has pulled her hair off the collar of her Burberry raincoat and tied it up into a chignon. The sound of her heels on the steps drowns out her words: 'Are you coming with me to Dijon?' I tell her I would rather stay with Dad and Lucien to make brawn. She does not reply but, at moments like this, when she catches my eye, I feel like a fish swimming around its bowl. The other day I was struggling with a multiplication table and she said to me in a curt voice: 'It's not that difficult.' It felt as if an ocean separated us in that second, even though we were side by side at the desk.

From the restaurant's dining room I can see Mum standing

on the station platform waiting for the local train to Dijon. She has sensibly knotted the scarf around her neck to protect herself from the kiss of the wind. I've got a lump in my throat watching her leave this way. Dad calls out to me: 'Come and eat your chips and calf's liver.' He knows very well that I'm watching Mum through the pane of the glass door. He grabs me by the collar: 'You call this helping to make the brawn? There's still plenty of work for you to do, kiddo.'

I hear the roar of the railcar leaving the station. When she goes like this on a Saturday, for a short moment I think she might never return. The thought makes me run into her bedroom and throw myself on her pillow to inhale her perfume. Then I can be sure she'll come back in the evening. There will be a book and a new pair of trousers for me, and she'll want me to try them on. I will be happy.

8

Lulu is in the middle of cutting up my calf's liver, while you are adding sizzling chips to my plate. I say I want 'Gravy! More gravy!' You answer me with one your favourite expressions: 'Hold your horses!' We are all eating at the work surface. You two are standing, and I'm sitting on a stool in between. It feels good, all of us men hanging out together. Nicole has just arrived for the service. She has been to the hairdresser. She has 'had her colour done' and she doesn't want anything to eat. You butt in: 'It's because she doesn't want to get fat.' 'Shut up, you horrible man,' she says, as she lays the tables.

On Saturdays at the Relais Fleuri you don't do a set menu. It's just a skirt steak and chips, prepared to order, giving you time to chat with the diners, who are not the usual weekly crowd. The workers, drivers and builders give way to a colourful assortment of market clientele, happy to get together when it's time for a glass of Aligoté wine or an aperitif like Meteor or Pontalier-Anis. You have the well-heeled gourmets who come to the market to buy their rack of lamb and Brillat-Savarin cheese for their Sunday lunch; the concierges – chatty as magpies – whose *pot-au-feu* will waft up the stairwell; the pensioners who grow enough vegetables to feed a regiment and have come to sell their three garlic bulbs and two winter cabbages; the militants from the Revolutionary Communist League and Workers' Struggle who argue together late into the night. Finally come the railway workers, between trains, who work on the maintenance of the railway lines. You like this little Saturday crowd who don't watch the clock. Aperitif time never seems to end for them, prompting Nicole to mutter about the dawdlers at the bar. She threatens them, telling them the steak will run out, to get them to sit down. But there will always be second helpings of the chips for the penniless students. You've never been rich, but you are always generous to a fault when it comes to those who don't have much.

Of your childhood, shrouded in silence, you only ever told me stories about other people. Like the one about the pedlar who always had a place at the table when he came to your little house, tucked away somewhere between the railway line and the forest. He carried a bundle which he'd open out on the kitchen floor. Your mother would buy more than she needed so he didn't starve. He'd have cheap trinkets, a religious image, flints and sewing thread. When the snow lent a pallor to the dusk, your father would make him sleep in the barn's hay and straw. One day, the pedlar offered you a strange dry, red fruit, which he said came from Africa. You bit into it then began to run, your mouth on fire. Everyone laughed at this first discovery of chilli, and you would often tell me about this misadventure while you were finely chopping the tip of an Espelette pepper into a terrine mix. We've both always liked the sharp taste of chilli. I introduced you to my 'anti-depressant' – my name for bread topped with harissa, a drizzle of olive oil and a crushed garlic clove.

Lucien lifts the lid of the brawn; you gently push the tip of a knife into it. Squinting, you say, 'It's ready.' Getting the pig's head out of the pot is akin to a piece of theatre, steam and heat everywhere. You place it on a thick circular section of spruce wood that serves as a carving board for your big pieces of meat. You've always liked to use the fragrant materials from around us to make kitchen utensils, like box tree for your pot handles and doughnut cutters. You inhale the juniper scent of your knife handle as you debone the head. As you do this, Lucien strains the stock, reduces it and adds parsley. You make sure not to lose one flake of the meat you're scraping off the bone. And you won't entrust the job of cutting it into narrow strips to anyone else. The creature's skull soon begins to appear, ivory and gleaming. I am hypnotised by its monstrous face. One day when I am older, Lucien will bleach one with soda crystals. I will go to school with my immaculate pig's skull for our object lesson. Afterwards the teacher will put it away on top of the cupboard next to an ammonite fossil.

You light a cigarette while the meat simmers in the thick stock. Lucien lines up salad bowls, dishes and jars on the stainless-steel counter. You grab hold of the ladle and fill them all with brawn. Lucien puts a jar on the kitchen windowsill to cool. You'll open them up this evening and, as usual, will say: 'Not bad, could have seasoned them more.' You're never satisfied.

Today it's something more. You're even more preoccupied, thinking about Mum in Dijon.

'You're going to Gaby's for the holidays,' you tell me.

'Lulu's brother?' I have never met him, but there isn't much I've not heard about him. I feel panic rising in me. 'Why?'

'You just are, that's it.' Don't make a fuss, you tell me. Everything will be fine.

It's the first time that I will be away from home. I'm delighted to be going to Gaby's house, but I'm scared I'm never going to see you together again. You and Mum.

9

It turns out to be the best holiday of my life. Gaby lives with Maria, whom he describes as being 'as beautiful as an angel'. She has incredibly round blue eyes, like buttons on a little boot. Maria makes beetroot soup that I can't stand. I console myself with her honey cake. Maria is Russian; sometimes she speaks French as if she has got pebbles in her mouth too, like the fishmonger.

I know the story of Gaby's life even before I get to his house. Gaby fought against the Germans. At first he went underground as part of the Resistance – the Maquis – in the Haut-Doubs, later joining the Moroccan Goumiers, or 'the Tabors', as they say with a mix of fear and admiration in the village. These soldiers served in units attached to the French Army between 1908 and 1956. Gaby never talks about his war; other people tell his story. In his wallet Lucien has a picture of his sibling sitting on a jeep mounted with a rifle. When he gets it out he says: 'You see, my brother fought the war with the Arabs and I fought against them. Figure that one out.'

One day I listened to Lucien tell you the story – and it wasn't for the first time – about Gaby meeting Maria. It is a night when he is in Germany and the Tabors have set up a bivouac in a village. Gabriel is off in search for wood for the fire when he comes across a terrified young girl shivering in the straw of a barn. At six foot two, Gaby has the physique of a man used to working the land, able to wield bales of straw easily with a pitchfork. Maria trembles at the sight of this terrifying-looking guy, a dirty sheepskin over his combat jacket. He approaches her and begins to speak to her. She does not understand him. He kneels down, bringing himself level with this shadow with frozen lips. Gaby gently removes his sheepskin and holds it out to her as she continues to shake with fear. He stands back and does a mime of a man coming back. When he eventually returns with some food and a blanket, she stares at him, her doll's eyes wide with surprise. He opens the American K-ration pack. He hands over the chocolate bar and crackers, which she eats. Gaby then sets about making a fire to warm her up. Behind him two guys are now standing at the door, laughing and saying he will 'have a good time tonight'. He tells them to 'go fuck yourselves'. All night Gaby keeps vigil over Maria, who is still too frightened to shut her eyes. From time to time he replenishes the fire and gestures to her to sleep. In the end he is the one to nod off at dawn, his gun between his legs.

The story that Lucien likes to peddle is that Maria and Gaby were never apart from this night onwards. People turned their nose up at her when they saw him come back from war with this girl speaking an unknown language and coming from among the communists. They said she was deported because she had sold her body in German factories. When he published their wedding announcement in the papers Gaby went into the village café. Before he bought everyone a round of drinks, he leant against the bar and warned: 'The next person who talks filth about Maria will be crying out for their mother in pain after I'm done with them.' Everyone kept their mouth shut.

Right from the start of the holiday I adore Maria and Gaby. When Maria takes me in her arms she smells of violets, not the complicated perfume of my mum. I watch her cut out patterns from magazines for her floral dresses. She listens to Ménie Grégoire's shows on the radio as she works away on her sewing machine, smiling when the radio host talks about sex. Gaby and Maria never seem to stop cuddling, even in my presence. It's like they're always attached. Even when Gaby is off cutting logs in the forest, it's as if he's by her side. For Maria Gaby built the house in Douglas fir logs, so she'd be reminded of the traditional *izba* log houses of her Russian homeland.

'It's my doll's house,' he says, surrounded by a sea of his wife's embroidery. Gaby and Maria do not have children. They have an unknown number of cats, all of which are called Kochka, which is Russian for 'cat'. Their house smells of wood and jam. I like the blackberry jam especially. Maria knows all the berries and mushrooms in the forest. She makes infusions with all sorts of plants, like bramble leaves with a bit of honey when I have a sore throat. I often 'find' a little scratch on me, so Maria will take care of me.

Their house consists of an L-shaped living room. They eat and sleep in it. Their bed is in the foot of the L, behind a thick, garnet-coloured curtain. I have my room – it's tiny – which is occupied entirely by a big mattress filled with corn leaves and a shelf on which Maria keeps her jams. Strings of dried mushrooms hang from the ceiling. Maria uses them to make her *pelmeni* – Russian filled dumplings – of which I very quickly cannot get enough. She teaches me to make them by folding over discs of pastry filled with stuffing into half-moon shapes, before carefully dropping them into boiling water. I go into the garden to pick the dill sprigs to mix with cream for the sauce to accompany them. One evening Maria tells me you can also stuff *pelmeni* with bear meat. My disgusted expression makes them both laugh. Gaby adds that he ate birds grilled on a wood fire as a child and even fed himself on fox when he was in the Resistance. 'That said, you do need to leave it outside to freeze before preparing it,' he explained.

Maria and Gaby have chickens, rabbits and a garden. With what they can find in nature, I get the impression that they are self-sufficient. When the baker passes by in his truck twice a week, they buy split *fendu* loaves, flour, sugar and coffee. Maria likes coffee a lot, which she drinks very sweet. When someone comes to visit, she always says: 'Let's make some coffee'. She's the one to make it in the morning and brings it to Gaby in bed. I'm allowed to sit between them at this time. We watch the sun blaze orange across the forest's dark silhouette. When it rises above the foliage Gaby will say: 'Come on, gang, time to get up!'

Gabriel describes himself as an anarchist woodsman, which in my childhood view of things can be summed up as two things: He never goes out without his chainsaw, and is always singing the anti-military song 'La Chanson de Craonne' at the wheel of his Renault 4L. He has been to war but hates – in no particular order – soldiers, priests, politicians and policemen. He will tolerate the gendarmes because one night, when Lucien got hammered on the hard stuff, the gendarmes pulled him out of a ditch and delivered him back to his mother. I like to sit in Gaby's Renault because I can pretend that I'm heading off to war. The car smells of petrol, engine oil and freshly cut wood. It also has machetes, axes, a poleaxe, wedges for splitting logs and some files for sharpening the chain of his saw. However, it's the heap of khaki rags on the back seat that conjures up war to me the most: combat fatigues, boots and a M43 jacket. I ask Gaby, 'What happens in war?' He scratches his temple and says: 'Eighty per cent of the time you're bored stiff and for the rest of the time, you're in the shit, big shit.' He turns the wheel sharply, steering into an area of ground to store logs roadside. I fidget on the Renault 4L's seat. We stop just before a deep rut filled with storm water.

Gaby tells me, 'You'll see, I'm taking you to a place I've cleared beautifully.' It smells of wet honeysuckle and moss-eaten wood stumps. We head across a springy stretch of grass to get to a clearing where the birch trees are bathed in rays of sunlight. Gaby has already felled and chopped several of the trees. He puts his chainsaw down so he can fill it with petrol and sharpen its chain. Sometimes he'll stop what he's doing and come out with lines as absurd as they are made up: 'Bakunin said a man should never be without two things that he must take very good care of: his willy and his chainsaw.' Then he shakes his head and rolls his eyes, exclaiming: 'My God who does not exist, how can I talk such rubbish? Just don't repeat this to your parents, OK?'

Lucien says about his brother that he cannot do anything without talking nonsense. Apparently, even in the war he would make the Germans laugh before shooting them. And Gaby has a very particular view of work: if it's something he *has* to do then he won't do it. One day, when we had stopped for a snack, he explained to me that 'once a job does my head in, I get another one. You won't catch me being a chef, that's for sure. And it's the same with love. The moment things started dragging with a woman, I'd be off. It's not the same with Maria, though. Just chopping small bits of wood for her stove makes me happy. And I love that she's in charge. When I watch her embroidering or knitting her things, I always feel like I'm seeing them for the first time. That's how you'll know as well. When you really enjoy doing these little things with a woman, you'll know she's the one.'

When he is not cutting wood, Gaby helps out with the harvest and making hay. He also kills pigs and makes boudin sausage. 'But he only ever gets paid money once in a blue moon,' says his brother, chuckling. Gaby has never signed up for any kind of social security or state pension, which he describes as 'a money trap by the mill masters to keep workers under their thumb'. When in need of something he pays the doctor and the pharmacist in quantities of wood, chickens and morel mushrooms.

Gaby loves, above all, his forest, 'where there is no God or master'. As he starts up his chainsaw, I'm still in the middle of going back and forth fetching tools from his Renault 4L. I pretend I'm getting cold so I can put on the M43 jacket, which comes down to my knees. I start the fire. It's sacred, fire, when you are in the wood. Gaby shows me a spot where I should gather twigs and bark. The flames are beginning to lick the little pyramid of logs that I have arranged. Gaby is watching me out of the corner of his eye. 'Don't overload it too much, your fire, or it will collapse.' Today he has cut down thickets of young trees crowded in too close together. 'The wood is good for making string, and bakers like it for getting their ovens going,' he explains to me. He lines up a first row of logs on dead leaves and asks me to continue stacking them. Now and then he interjects: 'Be careful, your pile of wood isn't lined up – it could all take a tumble.' Gaby is not like my father. He never loses his patience or raises his voice when I haven't understood him. I want him to be my schoolteacher. When I'm with him I want to learn. The names of trees and insects. Even calculations and geometry seem simple when he explains them to me with his little logs of hazel.

Between the fire and stacks of wood I don't feel like I've had a moment's rest. I am trying to work quickly to please Gaby. I am so hot I have to take off my jacket. He turns around. 'Easy does it, there's no mad rush.' With him it's never suddenly all go, like in the restaurant; unlike my father and Lucien, though, he is often on his own. 'It's what I prefer,' he says. 'I can barely put up with myself let alone anybody else . . . And anyway, there's always company in the forest.' I'm intrigued when Gaby talks like this. Lucien has told me Gaby talks to the trees and that, one day, a litter of fox cubs lay down on his M43 jacket as the mother watched on. I found out what a strange protector–wizard Gaby was when I went holly-picking with him. We'd followed a steep path until we reached a plateau of ferns and heather, where we came across an immaculately kept hunter's cabin. The door was unlocked. It was dark inside, with a strong smell of old tobacco and pastis. It had a table, two seats, a wood-burning cooker and a kitchen cupboard. Gaby opened a drawer and made a sign for me to be quiet. He gestured for me to 'come and look'. In the half-light, I saw five little baby dormice hibernating in a drawer in which Gaby had placed some straw and a torn rag. I went to touch them but he held my hand back. 'Leave them be or you'll wake them and they'll perish,' he murmured. He says 'die' for a human and 'perish' for an animal, but he wouldn't hurt a fly.

When the gnawing in my stomach becomes even more persistent after I've finished piling up a heap of logs, Gaby looks at me mischievously. 'You think you've earned your lunch, eh?' he says, putting down his chainsaw. He begins by getting a handful of potatoes out of his canvas bag and placing them onto the red-hot coals of the fire. He asks me to go and cut two very straight branches, the ends of which I must sharpen into points. He skewers bacon, rabbit thighs or chicken wings onto them, and at other times fish, kippers, those smoked, salted herrings which I only know as the silver and gold fish. I love to smell the smoke wafting up from the fire onto these fish spindles. I adore the way their oily warm flesh drips down and bastes the potatoes, turning them into a mash to which we'll add wild onion. And kippers make you thirsty. Gaby sloshes some light red wine into my glass of water. I feel like we are brothers in arms; we could have fought together in the Vosges or the Ardennes. I try and copy him when he eats chunks of bread with a knife. He assures me that herring is the sustenance of miners, workers and anarchists. I will have to explain it to you, Dad, as you make your terrine. Gaby fills his pipe with Scaferlati tobacco. 'You want to try it?' he says to me one day. With him nothing is forbidden but everything must be respected. 'That's what you call anarchy,' he says, offering me his little pipe. Anarchy makes me cough horribly. 'It's a good sign,' he decrees.

The afternoon that my parents are due to come and pick me up, Maria has made me as spick and span as a shiny new penny. She has washed my clothes, all now folded and packed in my little paperboard suitcase. It also contains a little bag of her jams and a book of pressed herbs I have made over the holidays. Maria has taught me to dry the plants between two pieces of blotting paper. Gaby tries to make me smile by saying I still smell of kippers. He tells me that, next holidays, he'll teach me how to use the chainsaw. Still the knot in my stomach won't go away. I go for a walk in the garden. I'm stroking a cat stretched out between two rows of beans when I hear the sound of the car. I have no wish to go and greet them. I can hear my father's foot-steps approaching and soon I am contemplating the tip of his black espadrilles. I raise my head, I am blinded by the sun, he takes me by the hand to help me up. He kisses me hello quickly.

He's got a few days' worth of beard flecked with grey. I stand back and see Nicole whispering with Maria behind him. 'What about Mum?' My father squeezes my shoulders. The silence between us seems to last forever. My mouth blurts out a question before I can even think about it: 'Has she died?' After a long sigh, he replies, 'No, of course not, why would you say that?' I am panicking, blinded by my tears. I don't hear his reply, I shout: 'Gone until when?' But I've already understood it's for ever.

PART TWO

PART TWO

I

When I wake up I say to myself that maybe she's still here, I just need to cross the hall to push open the door of her bedroom. In fact, I often have this dream. I stumble into the darkness, searching for the end of her bed. I climb up on the edge of the mattress and curl into her back. I stroke her heavy hair. I kiss it. She whispers into her pillow: 'Is that you, my darling?' She turns around, boiling with sleep and, as she embraces me, she murmurs, 'Give me a cuddle.' I pull my knees up to my stomach and rock back and forth. She smothers my back with kisses and says: 'Who's my lovely little boy?'

The white light of the day seeps through the shutters. We fall silent. Mum falls back asleep, snoring in fits and starts. My eyes linger on the mole of her right hand. I love this mole, like a mislaid piece of confetti on her olive skin. Sometimes, when she is correcting homework, smudges of red ink surround it. She also has a bump on her index finger. 'It's the pen mark,' she explains. For my father, 'It's the bump of knowledge.' Suddenly, my mother wakes up and rummages for her watch on the bedside table. 'It's seven a.m., darling,' she says, telling me to 'hurry up' in English. I like it when she talks to me in English, I feel as if we are in *The Avengers*. She has promised me: 'One day we'll go to London.'

It takes the sound of actual footsteps in the room to wrench me from this dream. It's Nicole's weary step. She often says her legs hurt, because of her varicose veins and having to stand fifteen hours a day in the restaurant. As she massages those purple veins on her ankles I sometimes forget her mature beauty, the sophisticated curls currently dyed platinum. When she smokes her Royale menthol cigarettes, seated at her cash register, poured into a pencil skirt, men sometimes forget the beer in their glass. Lucien says, 'She could make a Hussar regiment charge with swords drawn.' She tackles the boors at the bar with smart retorts that the regulars love. The other day, while she was washing glasses, a man said to her: 'How's it hanging, honey?' She immediately shot back: 'Way too high for a big jerk like you.' All the guy could do was stare into his Suze aperitif.

To blot out the pain I take out your recipe book. I retrieved it from the drawer of Mum's bedside table before Nicole moved into your bedroom. I often leaf through its pages under the sheets. I'm not really reading the recipes, I'm trying to find Mum in her handwriting. I linger over each and every one of the letters, imagining the mole on her finger as it holds a pencil. She has her own particular way of forming an 'e', finishing it with a stroke that leaps into the void instead of curving back. 'It's my rebellious streak,' she explained to me, laughing, one day. She asked me if I knew what a rebel was and, as I wasn't sure, she had suggested Zorro or Robin Hood, someone who helped the poor, acted alone and didn't need to show off. 'Like Dad,' I had declared. She had smiled.

When you announced to me that Mum had gone, you simply said, 'It wasn't working between us any more. Nicole will look after you now. With me.' From that point on, Nicole occupied your bedroom while you slept downstairs because you didn't want me to sleep upstairs on my own.

Not one single trace of Mum remains in this house. Gone are her books, her clothes in the wardrobe; her watch and Nivea cream no longer lie on the bedside table. Even her scent has disappeared. Sometimes I can't help myself, I long to find it on a pillow. All I ever find is the nauseating smell of Nicole's hair-spray in its place. In the bathroom Nicole has left a vanity case full of beauty products. She wears a lot of make-up, especially when she goes out on a Saturday night. You, Father, say she'll be 'stopping out' till Monday morning. You cannot stand her 'fella', André, otherwise known as Dédé. Smooth-talking and handsome, he wears a Prince of Wales check suit. His dark hair is slicked back with brilliantine when he comes for Nicole on a Saturday night. He waits for her at the bar, the only one to drink whisky, 'And just Chivas,' he'll say to puff himself up in front of the other drinkers, promising a third of them one in the order. He always has a business proposition. 'A barely driven BMW'; 'Suits like ones from the Italian designer Smalto', or 'Montrachet wine at knock-down prices'. He offers rounds at the bar that Nicole pays for. When he catches sight of you through the serving hatch, he vows never to eat here because it's like 'foreign rubbish' and, besides, he's a regular at the Restaurant du Parc 'with a Michelin star'. His presence is so intolerable to you, you tell Nicole that she can go early – you'll finish up the room and bar. You often say to Lucien you'd like to 'waste that lowlife' who comes to Nicole in the week to tap her for money. She knows you hate him, but she sighs and says, 'It's my Dédé'.

Lucien pulls down the iron shutter of the façade and says, 'See you on Monday.' You finish drying up glasses as I watch *Johnny Halliday's Greatest Hits* on the hanging TV by the bar. You bring me an Orangina and peanuts. You burst out 'It's Saturday night', but your voice betrays you. Finding ourselves alone together till Monday weighs heavily on you. You might well be whistling as you polish your cooker, but you cannot help but exude sadness from your every pore. I count the moments you don't have a cigarette in your hand or one slowly burning on the corner of the cooker. Your hair has gone grey and your hands are all wrinkled, now that Mum isn't here to massage them with cream. You never talk about her. It's as though she never existed. And yet I know she's everywhere in this house. You don't go upstairs any more. You leave it to Nicole to do the cleaning and tidying up there. The other day you told her off when she called me Juju, like Mum used to. 'He's got a proper name and it's Julien.' You never want to make brioche any more, or an orange salad done with flower water. You no longer buy oysters.

Sundays are tricky for us, but we cling to our rituals. We are like tightrope walkers moving through a life without Mum. We balance precariously, always at risk of plunging suddenly into sadness. Before going up to bed I catch you walking across the restaurant to sit at the table by the window, where Mum once came in for lunch on her own. Since she has left, no one ever eats at the table. Nicole is careful not to set it. It has transformed into a floral square of plants. A silent monument.

On Sundays, you wake me up at 9 a.m. with the pain aux raisins you've gone to get with your newspaper, *L'Est Républicain*. I eat breakfast in the kitchen, then do my homework next to you as you sit reading your paper and drinking your jug of coffee. You always start with the obituaries, then the small news items, finishing up with the local page. Sometimes you lift your head: 'What does "obsolete" mean?' I run upstairs to get the dictionary and come back down with the definition for you. You want me to make an effort as I read it out to you. 'Makes sense if you ask me,' you say. It's your particular expression when you learn something new. With Mum around, you never needed a dictionary to learn the meaning of a word, but you never dared ask her. Now that she's gone you want us to get all the knowledge we can together.

At 11.30 we go out together to get chicken and crisps at the butcher on the Grand-Rue. Opposite, in the patisserie, I choose a chocolate éclair, you a Paris-Brest. We walk down to the old town, across the canal, then walk alongside a hayfield to a path of poplars that disappears as it nears the river. There's not a soul on the gentle slope of the riverbank where we sit. The bell of the collegiate church rings noon. You open a can of beer for yourself and an Orangina for me.

I've lived through every season with you on these Sundays, in this patch of solitude. Chewing on a chicken leg, munching crisps, neither the rain nor the cold ever stopped us from coming. You take out your little transistor radio from your canvas bag (just like Gaby's) and tune it to Europe 1. After this you load my bamboo fishing rod with a tiny bit of chicken for bait. You prefer casting or fishing with spoonbait. I don't actually remember us ever catching much. It didn't matter. Sundays were when we could be together by the rustling poplars. On the radio, Michel Delpech is singing 'Flirt'. Personally, I prefer Kool and the Gang. Sometimes you look at me intently from head to toe, as if you've just seen me for the first time this week. Then you go back to looking at the line of your rod and you grumble kindly: 'Look at the state of your jeans. We must get you another pair.' I like it when you tell me off. It means you're taking an interest in me.

I count each passing hour rung out by the bell of the collegiate church. I tell myself that, before the next one, I'll ask you why Mum left without saying goodbye. I feel bereft, orphaned of words she could offer that could reassure me. She herself always said there was a reason for everything. The Earth turns around the Sun; female mammals have mammary glands; the Allies beat the Germans in 1945; leaves fall in autumn. That's why I need to know. I try to go over the images in my mind of our past life, but I get stuck at brioche on Sundays, the joy in your smile as we kneaded its dough together, the paella pan you put on the bed, serving Mum champagne and oysters. I get muddled trying to recall the words you two exchanged, muffled through bedroom walls. I can no longer see the colour of Mum's scarf when she waited for the Dijon train. I promise myself that at 2 p.m. I will ask you why she went away. The question gnaws at my insides. I need a magical act to make myself feel better: I pull my line out of the water and prick the flesh of my thumb with the hook. Blood forms into a droplet. It's blood money, just like in the adventures I dream up after reading the tales of the hero Rahan in the kid's comic book, *Pif Gadget*. You frown and ask: 'Why are you bleeding?' I mumble: 'It's nothing, I caught my thumb on the hook.' The bell rings two. I still haven't asked the question. I will wait till the next drop of blood.

Nothing bites on my line. I've barely got up when you start to worry: 'Where are you going?' You know very well that I am just going to walk up to the gravel, but another response burns my lips. I want to blurt out: 'What the fuck is it to you? You're not my mother!' I want to see you and Mum closing the door on me after shooing me out, like before.

2

The wind's kiss freezes my lower back as I kneel on the pebbles to pick up a piece of wood. I have always hated the north wind, particularly here in our home in the East of France. It's a dismal wail that blows across that slope of plains, lakes and forests trampled by history.

I show you a piece of wood polished smooth by the water. It has the shape of a cane. You suggest we refine it with your Opinel pocket-knife. I watch your deft blade making tiny shavings. Your dexterity fascinates me.

'How did you learn to do that?'

You smile. 'I learnt by watching the shepherds when I looked after the sheep. We'd make whistles from elderberry wood or a stylus to dip in ink and draw.'

You hand me my piece of carved wood. 'What will you do with it?'

'I don't know. I'll put it with the others in my room.'

'How about we use it in the kitchen?'

'In the kitchen?'

'To make vents in the pies and the pâté en croûte.'

'Are you sure?'

'Yes, why would I say it otherwise?'

I finish up the crisps while you take down our fishing rods. I don't like this moment when we have to leave; it reminds me I've got to go to school tomorrow and of the week to come. You'll be tied to the cooker, Nicole busy in the restaurant; routine will blot out everything. I want our life to be like in the Westerns. You'd be a scout in Comanche territory, a bounty hunter, a gold prospector or a trapper. We would ride off into the horizon, conquer the Wild West. We'd have ambushes on hills, shootouts in the desert and snowstorms in the Far North. My horse would be piebald, small and nervy; I would have a dog called White Fang that looked like a wolf. We would eat baked beans around the fire, where you'd sleep fully dressed, your hat tipped forward over your face. You would have cowboy boots like the biker who occasionally comes into the bar. You would also have a sawn-off Winchester like Josh Randall in the film, *In the Name of the Law*. You actually look a bit like Steve McQueen. You have his gaze, but you have such a short fuse. All it takes is a late delivery or a cold plate to set you off. Especially since Mum left.

Like every other Sunday evening, we go to the cheesemonger. To you, this lost farm atop a plateau of hazels and pines is known as the 'chalet'. The radio is burbling a boring political show you're not listening to. You just need noise. The road leads upwards in sharp bends. I like the twilight. In the evenings a restaurant is never still, just an endless round of activity till the early hours, always a bit of terrine or goat's cheese to munch and talk over. I breathe in the milky odour of the 'chalet'. Winter or summer, my feet freeze on its granite floor regardless. While you make your purchases I lean over the copper vat where the cheeses are made. There is also that strange tool, half rake and half broom, with steel bristles for cutting up the coagulated milk into pieces as small as corn kernels. Soon these will become the rounds of cheese or *tommes* – mountain cheese – whose scent I will inhale in the cellar. Here, in the half-light, I go up and stroke their rinds. They are damp, salty, feel like parchment. You choose a dappled Rondin whose surface falls away like dust when the cheesemonger rubs it. 'Look at it closely,' you say to me. I see tiny dots. 'They're spiders, they make the rind of the *tomme*.' One day, the cheesemonger thrust a bag under my nose that had the most dreadful smell. It was the dried rennet of milk-fed veal, the part of its stomach able to curdle milk. I forget my sadness. I see you have as well.

It's 7 p.m. now, time for crêpes. I'm the one to prepare the batter. Without a recipe, obviously. You are happy just to measure out the milk and the flour then melt the butter as I get my own utensils ready: a salad bowl and my little whisk, a smaller version of yours. I know how to crack the eggs properly in the flour now. After which I slowly add the mix of butter and milk. I whisk as vigorously as I can, as if the fate of the world depended on it. You stop me, saying, 'Not so quick, pay attention to your actions, do it more steadily or you'll get it everywhere.' You're laid back when you're not caught up in the lunch or dinner service. You have more patience. The stove is already roaring away, you always start it the night before, on Sundays, because you've always hated coming back to it cold on a Monday morning. I bang the crêpe pan on the stove's iron surface. 'Kid, don't ever strike the stove with anything, you're not respecting your tools.' In our home we never flip crêpes: 'That's for Mickey Mouse and his mates,' you say. I learn to turn them over with a spatula. They turn out like slightly burnt, torn handkerchiefs. 'Never mind, you're learning the job. Come on, let's start again . . .'

We have made a 'truckload' of crêpes because we'll have them on the Monday as well. I'm about to slather one with Maria's blackberry jam when you announce: 'Hold on, I'll show you something.' You take a saucepan, gradually empty caster sugar into it. When it melts, it smells of caramel. You take the saucepan off the fire, add some butter then some cream. You spread this mix on a crêpe. I sink my teeth into it.

'Not too bad, eh, my caramel sauce?'

For an instant it feels like nothing has changed. You're as happy as you were before. I turn on the television, the screen takes a few moments to appear. I announce the name of the Western: *Warlock*. I use my finger to make a circle on the plate and lick off the sauce. You pour yourself a draught beer. You sit next to me, a little foam on your upper lip. 'What about you, not having any?' You gesture no with your head as you sip your beer.

3

A warm breeze carries the scents of an Indian summer through the window. It smells of the golden leaves of plane trees in October. I hate this autumnal smell; it means it's time to go back to school. I hate the mauve of the crocuses growing along the riverbank where we go fishing on Sundays. I hate the monotony of your voice telling me to 'have a good day' as you're peeling onions. I hate the green velvet trousers Nicole has chosen for me, the dull smell of chalk on the blackboard when I am summoned up to it. I am currently contemplating some half-erased letters on its surface. I feel the whole weight of the class on my sore back.

'So, Julien, cat got your tongue?' Her voice has the effect of a sledgehammer on the back of my neck. My head jolts forward, narrowly missing the blackboard. It's always like this when Mrs Ducros talks to me. She is the nightmarish surprise of this school year. The new teacher of Year 6.

'We're waiting, Julien?' She looks at her watch again. I think at this moment I would rather jump off a cliff than utter a sound. I take out the recipe book.

My fingers slip beneath its leather cover. Mrs Ducros has asked us to write a story and read it out at the blackboard. The top-of-the-class student with a golden halo of hair has talked about his holidays in a caravan in Italy with his parents. He has told us all about the Romans, a volcano, the sea and how he dived into it. For someone like me he might as well have said that he'd been to the moon. I'm up straight after him; after Italy I'm talking about chocolate mousse. I could have talked about our Sundays together, the chicken, the fishing and the cheese at the chalet, but I was frightened others would steal what little we had left of our lives. I open the recipe book at the bookmarked page, I take a deep breath to cover the gurgling in my stomach and I leap into the unknown. I am making it up.

Above all, I cling to an image in my mind. It's of my mother, using her finger to lick a bowl of chocolate that you have melted. I want some too. Smiling, she says no with a shake of her head, then coats my lips with her index finger. You say: 'Stop now or there won't be any left for the mousse.' You whirl your mixing bowl around as you beat the egg white into peaks. They are so firm that you can stand your whisk in them. I narrate this in a loud voice while mimicking your actions. As I do in my description of the thick cream you blend into your mousse.

It's your little secret, always prompting the diners to ask how your mousse can be so creamy. You smile but never give it away, not even to your most loyal customers. I explain how people come to the Relais Fleuri just for your sautéed potatoes and chocolate mousse. At dessert Nicole sets down the bowl at the end of a table and each person helps themselves. I repeat your favourite phrase:

'Cooking is all about generosity.' You serve almond tuile biscuits the size of my hand with the mousse, for people to dip into their coffee.

I close the recipe book. I hear myself uttering, 'That's it.'

The heat emanating from the wood burner seems to make the silence even heavier. 'That's all?' The teacher asks.

I feel my schoolmates' embarrassment. 'It's made me hungry,' one of them tries.

Mrs Ducros is looking daggers at me. 'Absolutely nothing to do with the subject. That was a recipe, not a story.' She's really going for me now. 'I asked for French homework, not home economics.'

I am incapable of answering her. Yet I want to shout at her that cooking is the whole story of your life and I would rather learn the actions that you teach me a hundred times over than the endless learning by rote she metes out in class. I want to explain that each of your movements tells a tale; how your skill flows through the handle and blade of your knife. How you can knead butter with a bit of flour to – as you say – 'bring back' a sauce that is too liquid; how you can tell the exact heat of the stove simply by spreading the palm of your hand on it; how you can tell the age of beef by sniffing it.

'And the essay for this story?'

My hands tremble on the book as Mrs Ducros grabs it from me. She opens it at the chocolate mousse page. 'You've not even written anything. This is just a recipe. And on top of that, it's not your writing.'

She closes the book and throws it down. She's enjoying this. 'Give me your workbook.' She writes feverishly in it then snaps at me: 'This is to be read and signed by your father.'

I mull over what to do on the way back to the Relais Fleuri. I stride forward, stop, then retreat backwards. I try superstitious gestures: I touch the ground to convince myself that the world isn't ending. One moment I say to myself I will rush into the kitchen at full pelt, brandishing the book and admitting everything. I will tell you how I defended your chocolate mousse and your profession of cook, certain that you will approve. But this time, when I touch the ground, it feels as if it is giving away under me. I decide no, I won't tell you anything – but I still need your signature in my workbook.

Nicole stares at me as I walk across the bar: 'You look strange, Julien.' She is never one to try and prise information from me. She'll wait till we're all 'sitting down', then she'll say, 'A fault confessed is half redressed.' Not this time. My mouth is clamped shut. I go up to my room. I bury my head in the pillow. I want to cease to exist. One afternoon, when I was missing Mum unbearably, I shut myself up in my bedroom wardrobe. I wanted to stay in the dark for ever. I ended up falling asleep. Nicole found me. I remember her shock when she asked me what I was doing hidden away like that, and I'd answered, 'I'm killing myself.'

It's true that, since Mum left, you talk to me like you do Lucien. I feel like your commis chef when you ask me to peel potatoes or grate the Comté. Nicole seems unable to make up for the maternal tenderness I miss so much. She is awkward when she tries to be tender, as if she's struggling in a role. Living with you has cast me adrift in a world in which childhood has no place.

'Julien, come down for your hot chocolate.' Nicole has placed a bowl of it on the bar, along with some almond tuile biscuits. As I munch these, the plan comes to me. I will forge your signature by copying it from the bills in the folder under the bar. I will use your date stamp to make it look more real.

Nicole goes up to bed while you're 'getting ahead' with the *bourguignon*, which will taste even better when reheated tomorrow. I tell you I am going to watch television. I turn up the volume so you won't hear me. I open my workbook. On the left-hand page, I place a Relais Fleuri bill and, on the right, a piece of paper on which I practise copying your signature. I feel like I am floating on air. I don't feel like I am lying. I am protecting you from a primary schoolteacher's contempt. At no point do I fear your anger. I sign my workbook under the teacher's paragraph. I am exultant at the thought of tricking the silly cow. Even more so when I press the ink stamp down hard on the paper. Tonight I am exuberant as I kiss you goodnight. Too spirited, maybe, because your response is to say: 'Gently does it.'

The next day I feel confident about what I've done. My hands are steady when I hand over my workbook to Mrs Ducros. She observes the page at length, then asks me in a cold, mechanical voice:

'Why has your father added his restaurant stamp?'. Her words hit my brain like a storm of hailstones. I stare at the blackboard as if I'm looking for the vanishing point on the horizon. 'To make it look more real, right?' Nothing will make me open my mouth. I want to drop molten lead on her permed hair. I want her to be a man. It would be like in one of those action films, a kick in the nuts, a headbutt on the nose to watch it explode like a tomato, and a right uppercut under the chin. 'You're not going to answer me? As you wish then.' She grabs the workbook and stands up: 'Who wants to take this to Julien's father?' Everyone stares at their inkpot. 'OK, I'll pick a volunteer . . .'

Maybug walks before me. He is holding my workbook in both hands for fear he will drop it. We call him Maybug because it's more like a buzzing sound that comes out from under his thick mop of red hair than words. Intermittently he turns around and gives me a worried look. I've tried in vain telling him that I won't smash his face in because he's going to talk to my father. Maybug is not calm, even though I've made it clear I won't stop him, nor do anything to him. This is because Maybug is a 'poor waif', as Nicole calls him. He lives in a 'temporary town', made up of concrete cabins that smell of poverty, where the people shout a lot. And Maybug generally smells more of grease than washing powder. On the weekends we see him go by with a cartful of household bric-a-brac scavenged from dustbins. He goes begging at people's doors to try and sell it to the rag-and-bone man. On Saturdays he does the rounds after the market, retrieving bruised fruit and withered vegetables.

Maybug enters the restaurant. He mumbles something to Nicole. I am standing on the threshold. She turns and says, 'What have you done?' to me. I feel sorrier for him than worried for myself. I tell myself I am out on reconnaissance in Algeria and the patrol behind me depends entirely on my bravery. 'He has something for Dad to sign.' I am astonished myself at how calm my voice is: I'd make a good grenadier-skirmisher. Maybug disappears into the kitchen, Nicole hot on his heels. She has closed the door. Maybug darts out quickly, his head lowered. I help myself to a packet of nuts from the vending machine by the bar for him. He buzzes, no.

'Go on, none of this is your fault.'

I am alone in the restaurant dining room. I look at the clock to check time has not stopped. Dull thuds are coming from the kitchen. I'm beginning to get scared. 'Come here, Julien.' Your voice is calm and even. You're making paupiettes, flattening the escalopes with your rolling pin. Lulu brings you their stuffing. You address him, not me. 'Do you remember that time I put you in the clink in Algeria?'

'Yup.'

'You can't deny you'd been a fool, can you?'

'No doubt about it.'

'What was it like to be in the nick?'

'Nothing, I was just waiting for it to be over.'

'My superiors wanted me to punish you, but it was a waste of time banging you up, wasn't it?'

'Maybe. Don't know.'

You're slowly turning the rolling pin in your palm, while I'm thinking you're about to smash my sweet baby face with it. 'Go and wash your hands then come and get yourself to work. Now.'

You spread out an escalope on the cutting board. You place a large dollop of stuffing on it, fold the sides, rolling it up with string into a cross shape. It's down to me to do it now. My first paupiette bulges and the string is too loose. The second one lacks stuffing and looks like a trussed-up mummy. By the third, I'm beginning to get the hang of it.

'It's easier to string along your dad than string up a paupiette, isn't it?'

Silence.

'Answer me.'

'Yes, Dad.'

'What's all this about a recipe book?'

'It's the one Mum gave you.'

It's the first time I have said the word 'Mum' in your presence since you told me she'd gone. You stand back abruptly, light a Gitane and kick the door to the back courtyard. You tap its wooden frame and say, 'Bring me that book.'

I'm looking at you, clutching the book's leather cover to my jumper. 'Give it here.' You open the stove door. The coal is glowing red, a wave of heat envelops me. You throw the book into the oven but, just as quickly, Lucien retrieves it, his fist reddened and smelling of grilled pig. He comes right up close to your face and very slowly says: 'Don't you think you've been enough of an idiot already?'

4

The geraniums have turned the terrace of the Relais Fleuri purple. Every evening Nicole waters them with a yellow Ricard jug. She has laid out piles of my clothes on the bed and is loudly counting them. 'Make sure you change them regularly, OK?' Yes, I shout from the bathroom, where I am squeezing a magnificent spot in the mirror. I use this opportunity to put my hand into my pants and stroke the three hairs that have sprouted around my testicles. It's not that I'm particularly proud of them, I am just constantly intrigued by what is happening to me. No one will talk to me about my changing body.

After some bitter negotiation I am going off to holiday camp. In previous years I have helped you in the kitchen in July, then gone to stay with Gaby and Maria for August. For as long as I can remember, I've never seen you take a holiday. Although I do have this image that sometimes comes back to me, a photo on Mum's bedside table of all three of us at the beach. But the photo has disappeared. Just like the recipe book. Vanished, ever since Lulu stopped you sending it to hell in the fire. Several times I asked Lulu what had happened to it. He shrugged his shoulders and replied: 'What do I know?'

The Relais Fleuri stays open all summer because of the tourists who pass through the train station. If you have to close it for a few days, it's because the place needs work. You have made me promise that I will help you, Lucien and Gaby to redecorate the kitchen.

It will take us an hour and a half by railcar to get to the old farm. The station yard has been invaded by rucksacks and bikes. My bike, smaller than the others, is weighed down with my luggage. It is threatening to flip backwards unless I press down hard on the handlebars to keep it steady. I tried – unsuccessfully – to explain to you that I needed a bigger bike, but you weren't having any of it.

On platform 1, the railcar is humming. It's a beige and red Picasso train with an elevated control cabin for the driver. Two railway guards help us load our bikes. A camp instructor appears. He is called François and owns a splendid silver Peugeot demi-course sports bike. He tells us all about the hikes we'll take, the nights and evenings we'll spend in tents or around the fire. Nicole and you approve of all this but I'm not listening. I feel awkward in the midst of this group. The other boys all know each other and talk together about past holidays. The station master asks us to get on the train. Nicole kisses me. You move forward to kiss me, then suddenly say I'm old enough to shake your hand now. You smell of pastis. When it comes to getting drunk I only know the 'boozers' – as you call them – who hang around the Relais Fleuri wreathed in Gauloises smoke. They are never nasty and, when they get too noisy, Nicole asks them to 'tone it down'. They like to have a friendly pint, a glass of wine or an anisette. You've begun to linger with them. I don't like your new habit of drinking.

You end up giving me a quick peck as I stand on the train's running board. You step back down quickly onto the platform.

You know that I know about the alcohol. The train sets off. All the seats are occupied by groups of friends who are talking among themselves. I stay out on the open platform at the back of the carriage. The train regularly pulls into tiny country stations; the air smells of cut grass. I am fascinated by the driver up on his little perch, his dangling legs banging the pedals that control the engine. The Picasso's train horn sounds as it reaches the first plateau. Pine forests have replaced the prairies and darkened the horizon. The air has cooled. The railcar stops in the middle of nowhere.

'It's like Siberia here when you come in winter,' François tells me as I get my bike off the train. He comes from Dijon. Maybe he has seen my mother?

We cycle like a symphony of noisy crickets, a disorganised battalion. We shout, laugh and overtake each other. François and the other camp instructors stand upright on their pedals, trying to keep order in our platoon, but it's hopeless. I discover the fun of being in a pack of boys. The old farm where we are staying looks like a nave, a stone structure boarded up on either side with rusty corrugated iron. A bent iron staircase has been tacked on for a safety exit. The window-frames and doors have been painted green. On the ground floor a low-ceilinged room, like an old stable, serves as the dining room. Upstairs a row of sinks below high windows leads to a dormitory with a cracked wooden floor. The beds are slotted tightly between the wardrobes, some of which have doors that no longer close. Different groups take over their own little areas on orange bed covers that are the colour of the Ponts et Chaussées highway trucks. I find a bed near the escape exit, relieved to be set apart a little. I have no desire to participate in the full-scale assault of the wardrobes to store belongings, I prefer to stuff my rucksack under the bed. Suddenly an electric guitar riff booms out from black-painted speakers on top of the cupboards. Jimi Hendrix is among us, followed by French prog rock band Ange, and Maxime Le Forestier.

Life in the camp is merry chaos. Right from day one, I explain to François that I help in my father's restaurant and I can cook every day. I press hard by offering to make the bolognese sauce for the pasta. 'The dish that always comes to the rescue', you'd say when you felt lethargic. François looks at me sternly: 'You're not making this up, are you? You sure you know what you're doing?' I'm already so busy peeling onions that I can only answer him with a nod of my head. I grab a piece of pine log to use as a cutting board. I thinly slice the onions *à la paysanne*; I crush garlic cloves, dice the carrots, brown it all off. François brings me a pile of frozen meat. 'It's mincemeat.' I turn my nose up at it because, at our place, we make a bolognese sauce with a good piece of minced chuck steak. I let it all simmer for a few minutes, then add tomato purée and a tin of peeled tomatoes. I find beef stock cubes in the sideboard. I dissolve them in hot water to pour into my sauce. I add salt and pepper. I proffer a wooden spoon to some of the boys who are watching me, mesmerised.

'Try some!'

They close their eyes in pleasure. 'It's really good.'

I taste it too and, with an authoritative tone that makes François smile, I say: 'It still needs something.' I search in vain for some herbes de Provence and bay leaves. This is clearly not a camp for gourmets. On arrival I remember seeing the wild thyme on the roadside that I've watched you pick for your rack of lamb. Never mind that it's growing close to the tarmac. I rinse it quickly under the tap and finely chop it for my sauce. I taste again. 'Better,' and then I say those words of yours: 'Now, we have to forget all about our bolognese on the stove.'

At lunch my reputation is sealed. Not only have I managed to get my campmates to eat a grated carrot salad, thanks to a vinaigrette livened up with shallots, but I've also got everyone clamouring for second helpings of the bolognese. I am exultant seeing the plates licked clean of every last piece of spaghetti. From here on in I am called 'chef', although François cannot understand why I content myself with a bit of bread and Camembert. I reply proudly: 'Cooks don't have time to sit down and eat.'

One day I go blank about a recipe for one of your menu dishes. It's for hunter's chicken casserole. I ask if I'm allowed to call you. You are horrified to learn there are no professionals in the kitchen and demand to talk to the head of the camp. François tells you that my cooking – with the help of my campmates – is proving a treat for everyone. I can hear you getting annoyed on the phone. A few minutes later you call back: 'Write down what I'm going to tell you.' As I write, I feel as though the recipe book is coming back to life under my fingers. I wangle some white wine out of the instructors for the sauce.

My greatest feat is one I pull off during a trek. We are camping out in magnificent wilderness, a mountain stream hurtling by. In the field where we are setting up our tents, I curse at the rocks that jut out of the ground and make it impossible to secure my pegs. But worse is to come. The head instructor claims to us the end of the world is imminent and we must learn to survive with what we've got to hand. We do this by making outdoor furniture using just baler string, an axe, a knife and some hazel branches. The experienced camp regulars build tables that are masterpieces, benches, and even a draining rack for their battery of kitchenware.

One morning we are woken by clucking. A flock of lively

chickens has descended upon our tents. The headteacher explains our mission is simple but will be a key one for us as survivalists: we must come up with the best possible grilled chicken for lunch. But before we can even start, we have to stun the creature, pluck it, gut it and so on. Even the most daring of us is dubious at the prospect of this. Chasing chickens is one thing – and it proves to be a hilarious combination of rugby union and rustic corrida – but after that? A bloodthirsty lad grabs an axe and makes a go at decapitating a creature, with several pathetic attempts. I try to summon up my memories of slaughtering a chicken behind the *izba* log house with Gaby. I know you have to tie string around a live chicken's feet and hang it upside down to make it bleed from the neck. Our russet-coloured chicken thrashes about under an ash tree while the sharpest knife in our possession does the rounds of our group, eliciting no takers. Everyone is looking at me. I am the cook, so I must be the one who should kill it. I stroke its feathers the same way I've seen Gaby do, then slice its artery in one go. The blood drains into a large red pool on the grass beneath the shuddering creature. 'It's its nerves,' a boy says. I realise I've forgotten to make the fire for the saucepan of water. Everyone rushes around to cut little bits of wood and gather twigs. The fire gets going quickly. I don't explain anything to my campmates. They repeatedly ask: 'Can we help?' I ask them to go and pick wild thyme. I plunge the chicken in boiling water, just enough for the feathers to fall away when plucked. I gut it, put the giblets aside and stuff it with the wild thyme. My campmates have carved two wooden forks to hold a spit made of hazel. We take it in turns to roast the chicken. We present it to the instructors on a bed of gentian leaves.

I wanted you to be there on the last night when we made a

mountain of crêpes. My back and arms went numb. My camp-mates gave me a chopping board with my name carved on it.

The night I get home I drink a toast with you, Nicole and Lucien on the terrace. You ask me all about the hikes, the mountain passes we went through and the sites we visited, but all I want to talk about is cooking. You don't like it. You look away. Nicole puts down a plate of tomatoes covered with slices of white onion on the table. 'Tonight, with this heat, we're eating cold.' You uncork a bottle of *vin gris*, that very pale rosé you drink in the summer. You cut short the story of my exploits, putting your hand on Lulu's arm. 'Tomorrow the guys are coming to take away the cooker and install a new one.'

Lulu doesn't flinch. He cuts himself a bit of andouille sausage which he eats with a knife and some bread, like Gaby.

'We couldn't go on with the coal, it was no longer heating up; the stove is completely knackered,' my father persists.

'But if it's still working all right . . .' Lucien protests

You pat him on the back and talk to him as if you're in an advert.

'You'll see how gas is flexible and practical. No more having to divvy up the work of bringing up those buckets of coal from the cellar.'

Nicole approves: 'You have to admit that gas is cleaner. Besides, you're getting a bit old for lugging those heavy sacks.'

Lucien is not listening; he is rolling a cigarette with one hand on his thigh. The flame of his lighter accentuates the gauntness of his face in the half-light. I've stopped talking about my spaghetti bolognese and chicken. I thought you'd be proud of me but not so: as far as you're concerned, I have clearly spent my holidays cooking behind your back. It's worse than if I had misbehaved.

5

Lucien and my father returned from Algeria with one word: *mektoub*. Destiny. They put *mektoub* in all their sauces – for the football results, the neighbour's breast cancer and victory for Valéry Giscard d'Estaing in the presidential election. Yet Lucien is not happy about the *mektoub* that has befallen the soon-to-be-departed coal stove. He tells my father that one more time before getting on *la bleue*. He has overdone the gentian aperitif that leaves your throat parched and rasping long after the hangover has faded. He is rolling yet another cigarette to smoke on the road. He is drunk. Before getting on his moped he goes into the kitchen one more time to stroke the condemned cooker. If its old cast-iron sides could talk, it would tell a tale of never-ending vol-au-vents, flank steak with shallots and frogs' legs. It would tell you all about these two men's hands riddled with burns, the fire that would roar in its depth at dawn under a cauldron of cold water. It would describe the froth on the *pot-au-feu*; the heady scent of Mont d'Or cheese roasting in *vin jaune* and how the chicken skin puffed up and browned. Lucien knows all of this. For him, losing the cooker is like losing a parent. He is being orphaned.

Around midday the guys have finished moving out the cooker. They say, 'Now, you don't see cast iron like that any more.' They were not even born when the coal stove was installed. My father and Gaby have begun to wash down the walls for painting. Lucien has not arrived. 'His carburettor has bust,' says his brother, chortling. Everyone knows Lulu does not want to see 'his' cooker go.

I start a barbecue in the back courtyard. I am sweating as I saw away at grapevines. You explain to me that nothing is better than vine shoots for grilling food. 'As for everything else, since you were such a star chef this summer, you'll know what to do,' you say, going back to your work. You smile at me; your irritation of the night before has gone. I am overjoyed. I've got slices of pork rib the size of paddles at the ready. I vigorously spin the salad basket, sending water droplets splattering against the wall. I chop the chives. The table is set. So far, so good. You, Gaby and the workers sit down for an aperitif. You have positioned yourself at the end of the table so you can watch me cook, munching peanuts and drinking a Pontarlier. Still, you're careful not to interfere. I place the slices of pork rib on the barbecue. I turn the potatoes that stick to the grill. I can hear the sound of meat fat sizzling as it lands on the embers, but it's only when I turn around that I see the fat has erupted into flames. I move the pork ribs out of the way, flip the potatoes, which are clearly now doomed to being black on one side and raw on the other. I look to see if you are watching but you quickly turn your head to talk to your neighbour. I mix the green salad and vinaigrette together and put it on the table, hoping for a few minutes' grace while it's eaten.

But you, acting oblivious, ask the workers if they would like the green salad with the meal or beforehand. 'They are hungry enough to ask for it all on their plates. After all that glory, here comes my total downfall. You know this, but you don't do a thing to get me out of the situation. The ribs are burnt on the outside, raw on the inside. The potatoes are sticky or uncooked. The guys say it tastes delicious but they're being polite. You pick at your plate with the tip of your knife, a wry expression playing on your mouth. 'Go on, make us a nice cheese plate to finish off the salad.' I rush into the pantry and you come and join me. I feel ashamed. You rest your hand on my shoulder: 'You know, with cooking, nothing is ever guaranteed. One day you can be good, the next day average, all because you got out of bed on the wrong side. I know you did your best. In this job you learn by your mistakes. What's most important is consistency.'

The workman is welding the pipes that will supply gas to the new cooker. Lucien has finally showed up. He contemplates the scene, his face even more ghostly pale than usual. The workman has lent me a pair of protective goggles so I can watch him closely. He lights the blowtorch, which makes a whistling noise as he applies it to the pipe. Its little blue flame dances on the copper as he applies a metal ring to it to solder the join. He calls this 'brazing'. These words are like music to my ears. 'Dusting' the meat for when you sprinkle it with flour; turning crustaceans 'as red as a cardinal's robe' for when you put them back on a high heat, and 'winnowing' a sauce with a spatula to stop it developing a film. I love it when you are contemptuous of food processors, calling them 'threshing machines', or when you say you're looking for 'a black cat in a coal cellar' because you can't find something. As we all work away in the kitchen, you will often say to us: 'Tell me it's not caught up?' In your glossary, 'caught up' means many things: stuck to the bottom of the casserole, overcooking in the frying pan, boiling too quickly, lumps forming in the pancake batter . . . 'Caught up' is the most precious thing you have bequeathed me.

The four of us – you, Lucien, Gaby and I – are standing

contemplating the new cooker. You announce solemnly: 'We've got to break it in now.'

Gaby bursts out laughing and says: 'Just like with guns and women. It has to lose its virginity.'

On its beige enamel surface the manufacturer has affixed a plaque engraved with 'The Relais Fleuri'. You have filled your two-handled pot with water and put it on the gas. You are completely convinced: 'You can't deny it heats things up much more quickly.'

You turn on the oven; you rub its immaculate cast iron. Lucien stands a good distance away from it, his arms folded. You ask him to make a shortcrust pastry. I pit the damsons. You scold me because I'm not doing it quickly enough.

'Are you sure you've not forgotten something?' Lucien whispers to me.

I contemplate my beautifully arranged fruit, their pitted flesh facing up. 'What?'

'The semolina on the bottom of the baking tin, to mop up the juice of the fruit. Or your tart will be as soggy as a wet rag.'

I take it apart, sprinkle a layer of semolina on the pastry, put the damsons back into position then add a layer of brown sugar on top.

You are destroying the Brassens song 'Chanson pour L'Auvergnat'. You are as happy as Lucien is sombre. You send me to fetch some potatoes from the pantry. It's getting heated between you two upstairs. I wait for the storm to pass. You are like those old couples who squabble over TV programmes but start to fret if the other has been gone for a piss too long. You open the oven door: 'Pass me the sugar; got to perk up these damsons a bit more.'

You pull the tart out of the oven. The damsons have gone seriously brown.

'Looks like they've really caught the sun,' Lucien wagers.

'Happy now? It's the gas's fault!'

I feel a man among them. And it's got more to do with the fact I can do what they do than my recent discovery of the labia minora and majora, courtesy of the well-thumbed pornographic photo-story, *Lesbian Orgy*, that did the rounds in the camp dormitory. You share a bit of the tart with us, along with the last of a bottle of Rasteau wine. I'm juggling the handle of the frying pan in one hand, my glass in the other. The wine excites my taste buds after the tartness of the plums. I'm a little hot but I feel strong, confident in myself, now I'm a proper working man, putting grub on the table. And then, suddenly, a wave hits me: I want Mum to be here. I want her to call us 'my boys' and for you to do your 'posh bird' thing by serving her champagne. I emulate your actions to snap out of it. You turn towards Lucien: 'What about doing us a little omelette with those mushrooms you've brought?'

You take my hand. 'Come with me.'

You lead me into the backyard where we sit down, glasses in hand. In the twilight, you blow a large puff of Gitanes smoke saying: 'Leave Lulu to it, he's getting used to the cooker.'

You sip the wine in silence. Lucien appears with the omelette. 'What about the table, for Pete's sake! Leaving that to me as well, are you?' he says, chuckling.

You catch his arm. 'Julien, bring us a baguette and a knife. Let's eat with our hands like we're in the backwoods. We can use slices of bread and our fingers to pick up the omelette. Do you remember in Algeria, Lulu?'

Lulu acquiesces, filling our wine glasses. I feel your relief. Lulu and the gas cooker are going to be fine.

6

A young woman presents herself at the bar. She is selling the encyclopaedia *Tout l'Univers*. Nicole listens politely to her while flicking through one of the red-covered tomes. You observe them from your serving hatch, then come out of the kitchen and invite the woman to sit down and tell you about it. You turn the pages, nodding your head. You learn that the Spartans fed themselves on pig's blood and vinegar. You make a face at this. I'm already deeply absorbed in *Tout l'Univers* but now and then I observe you. She has cadged a Gitane off you. Her straw-coloured hair is cut very short. You ask her if it's difficult, selling books door to door. She says people are nice but they don't buy much. You look at me and ask: 'What do you think of *Tout l'Univers?*' I say 'great', continuing to read. You say: 'Bingo!' and the young woman is relieved: 'Do you really mean that, are you going to buy my encyclopaedias?' She needs to talk. She is trying to continue her studies. The encyclopaedias mean she can live and look after her baby. She's a young 'unwed mother', as people said back then. The father was a squaddie passing through, who promised her the moon then left after his military service. She takes out a picture of her little girl. You smile. It's late and she has to go and pick up the baby from her mother. You pull the steel shutter closed as if it's a full stop.

I never saw you with a woman who wasn't Mum. It was like the spark of romance died in you the day she left. Nicole once said, 'You need to find yourself someone nice. For the kid as well.' You muttered a no that seemed to be an end to the matter. I think I prefer it this way.

Overnight you learn that Lucien has skidded on a sheet of ice on his way home. His right leg is all bashed up. He must keep it immobilised for at least a week. You do the rounds of your acquaintances to find a temporary pair of hands. I pray to the patron saint of cooking that you don't find anyone because, as far as I'm concerned, I am Lulu's replacement. You don't manage to find anyone. The next day is a Sunday. Chicken by the river is out of the question. Together we must get ahead preparing dishes for the days to come.

You inspect your pantry and sketch out your menus on the kitchen counter. We tackle the beef and carrot stew first, so it can simmer away on the cooker for the rest of the day. Your stews have taught me to respect the value of time, how to work best with it. When I ask you if a beef and carrot stew needs a stock, a base or a gravy, you get irritated and say: 'Beef and carrots – it's obvious from its name.'

The black iron casserole is your vessel of choice for slow cooking. In it you tell me to brown the cubes of meat – but not too much – with onions or shallots, and to add carrots sliced into coin shapes, along with bay leaf and thyme. Then I must leave it to simmer with the lid on. I can't hide my surprise: 'That's all?'

'When a woman is beautiful she doesn't have to tart herself up,' is your reply.

I point out that Nicole wears a lot of make-up. You sigh and laugh: 'That's because she thinks the more make-up she wears, the more she'll be able to hold onto that bloke of hers.'

In your cellar lies a treasure which you guard jealously. Only you are permitted to open your salt chest, the impressively sized earthenware jar where you keep the pork charcuterie that is able to transform your *petit salé aux lentilles* – dry-cured pork with lentils – into a thing of joy. You have just come up carrying a shoulder of pork and some ham knuckles; you wash off the salt under a jet of tap water. You were born into a world where self-sufficiency was the only way not to starve. You have passed this taste for preserves on to me. I've scrubbed a few, those buckets of pickles, to drop into vinegar and salt. I have deseeded tomatoes by the wheelbarrow to make sauce. I've pricked basket-fuls of cherries with a pin so they can be preserved in eau de vie for an unadulterated treat. You have taught me how a season can be embalmed by drying chanterelle and black trumpet mush-rooms on a string.

I pierce an onion with two cloves and place them, together with a bouquet garni, in a large pot of cold water in which the pork shoulder and ham knuckles will cook for an hour and a half. During this time I prepare the lentils.

'Did you put salt in the water?'

'Yes, of course.'

You sigh: 'Don't you remember that you only put salt in with dried vegetables at the end of cooking? Or they become hard.'

You ask me to brown the onions and carrots. 'Now add your salt pork and the lentils and pour in a bit of their sauce. Not too much now, otherwise you'll waterlog it. Go on, a bit more . . . now stop, that's good. From you I learnt that less can be more. I peel the lemons carefully, without exerting too much pressure, so as to retain the zest, then press them to extract the juice. You talk to me about your periods of leave in Algiers with Lucien, when you tried *crépon*, a sorbet made with lemon. You also tell me how much you enjoyed omelette made with mallow, the plant that flowers on the roadsides and in fields.

You take out your lemon tart from the oven and put in an apple one. You lift the lid on the beef and carrots and stick your knife into a piece of the chuck steak. 'It's done. I'll reheat it tomorrow.'

All week I get up at 6 a.m. I peel potatoes before going to secondary school. In the evenings I dash off my homework as quickly as possible so I can throw myself into making macaroni cheese and baked potatoes. When Lucien returns the next Monday he says to me: 'So, I hear you worked your socks off.' You have not said a word to me. You don't know how to give praise; others must do it for you. Yet all of this gives me confidence. My mind is made up, I'm going to leave school and get a cooking diploma. The careers adviser is dubious when I talk to her about it. She says I should continue onto the baccalaureate at the very least because I'm a pretty good student. It will open doors, she tells me, including the world of hospitality. Back then, jobs in a kitchen were considered a dead-end. I dig my heels in. I know there is a good high school which teaches hospitality barely thirty kilometres away. I could even come back on the railcar in the evenings. 'We will have to talk about it with your father at the parent–teacher evening.'

Ever since the summer when I cooked at camp, we have made a pact, you and me. I'm only allowed near a pot when I have finished my homework and my grades and school reports are satisfactory. Sometimes I can be found reading near you in the kitchen, particularly when service is going on for ever. I take a book with me to the riverbank every Sunday. All of this convinces you that I'm a serious student. And it's true, I devour each and every book since you bought me *Tout L'Univers*. Often, when I am about to read, sitting at the counter, you ask:

'What's that about?'

'The Spanish Civil War,' I tell you.

I'm reading *Man's Hope* by Malraux. Our French teacher has set the bar high. For as long as I can remember, I have been enthralled by stories of war. Later on I'd often forget to sleep because I was reading Vasily Grossman's *Life and Fate* or *Wooden Crosses* by Roland Dorgelès. I am less inclined towards mathematics. I settle for reproducing formulas and geometric figures of which I have little understanding.

One day a salesman passed by. He extolled the virtues of ready-çooked chips, which he told you would save you time. You looked at him as if he was from the moon. 'In my book, chips mean potatoes, a knife, oil and some salt. That's it.' The sales representative looked ashamed and said: 'People like you, you see them less and less.' You burst into laughter and looked him up and down, as if he were peddling snake oil.

Tonight the restaurant is closed because we are off to the parent–teacher evening at my secondary school. You shave in the kitchen because you never use the upstairs bathroom any more. Although you've built yourself a DIY shower by the clients' toilets, you often clean up at the kitchen sink. You have promised me you'll teach me how to shave. At the moment, it's the acne on my chin and between my eyebrows that really stands out. You lather the soap with your shaving brush in the bowl. You could be whisking egg whites into peaks. I love studying your safety razor, which you maintain with the same care as you bestow on your knives. You shave with measured, elegant movements, punctuated by little taps of your razor in the sink to rinse it. I admire your calm, your light touch as the radio blares away. When you stand like this, bare-chested in front of a little piece of mirror hanging from the shelf, I feel that nothing bad could happen to us. You are my adventurer of a father, the pasha of the Relais Fleuri; my dad, who can do everything with his hands. You tell me to come and stand by you.

'Turn around.' You coat my neck with soap, and I feel the precision of your razor as it glides up my neck. I like the feel of the lather and the metal. 'There you go, you had three whiskers and some fluff that needed to go.' I would have liked you to offer me your razor and shaving brush to do my whole face, but you always say: 'There's no rush.' Lucien, on the other hand, lets me ride his moped to go and get the bread.

You have put on a white shirt ironed by Nicole. We make our way over there on foot. You stop to light a cigarette.

'So, which "bac" are you going to do?'

I've been waiting for him to ask what I intend to study for so long that it's been like holding a hot potato without knowing what to do about it. I decide the shortest possible answer is the best way forward.

'I want to be a cook.'

You let the flame of your lighter burn for what seems like an age. Your face in profile becomes tense. You have a face like a sad, wild animal when you turn to look at me. 'Don't do that, son.' You are puffing furiously on your Gitane.

'Why not? Am I not pretty good at it?'

'It's not that.'

'Then what is it?'

'I had no choice but to work with my hands. You, you've got a chance to learn.'

'But I learn with you.'

You sigh. 'Yes, but not from books.'

Our feet echo on the pavement. I am cold. I put my hands in my trouser pockets.

You put your hand on my shoulder and say: 'You know, when I started at the bakery, I was such a wee thing I would practically tip over into the kneading trough. Carrying those sacks of flour was back-breaking. And I'd get burnt by the hot ash. Now you, you should go to school for as long as possible, so you don't find yourself on some factory line or heaving heavy bags of cement on a building site. Learn a good profession.'

'But cooking is a good profession.'

'No, kid, you're not in the real world yet, you're shielded by me and Lulu. Go and see how it really is somewhere else. They'll shout at you, smack you, get drunk at the bar while you apprentices are sweating blood. And it's not a life, cooking. You're on your feet from seven in the morning till midnight. Even if it's going well, you always have that anxiety about the restaurant being empty, the service going tits-up, the kidneys or the blanquette not turning out right the next time.'

'But I like cooking.'

'Don't make it your life or it will eat you up. Learn a good profession.'

'What is a good profession for you?'

As we walk, he lists on his fingers, 'Accountant, industrial designer, engineer, doctor, railway worker, teacher. Civil servant – yeah that's a good one; you've got guaranteed employment, and nobody can take the piss like they do in the private sector.'

'Gaby said you have to be free to do what you want, and public sector workers are all collaborators.'

'Gaby doesn't give a damn about anything because he's lived

through war. In war, when you get up in the morning, you don't know if you'll still be alive at lunchtime.'

'But you know about war too.'

'That was different. I didn't have to liberate my country. Come on, let's talk about something else.'

We arrive at the school entrance at the same time as my form teacher. My father awkwardly shakes his hand, saying: 'I'm Julien's father.' As if it wasn't obvious.

7

For the umpteenth time I sketch a line on the tracing paper in Indian ink. I am supposed to be drawing the casing of a little electric motor. I have done a sketch using mechanical pencil and above all a lot of erasing, because I keep getting lost in my attempts at representing perspective. My pen strays from the lines. I've scraped away so many of my blunders with a razor blade, I've ended up making a hole in the tracing paper. I get annoyed and tear up the drawing. It's even harder to start all over again, given that I can't see any point in the industrial design and mechanical manufacturing that occupies entire days at school. A classmate has drawn Droopy the dog on the back of my overalls, which perfectly sums up my attitude in this first year of high school, specialising in mathematics and technical studies. I opted for this hideous concrete block planted in the middle of a priority social housing zone for all the wrong reasons: I thought it would stop my father insisting I pursue more education and I could focus on cooking. But it's a nightmare to come to this institution every day. When I leave my bike near the gymnasium and I contemplate the workshop's glass windows, the same thought always assails me: hold tight.

From this time one smell remains that I can immediately

summon up with a click of my fingers: machined hot metal. I am in the changing rooms. I open my metal locker; I take off my parka and put on my overalls. I take out my spanners, my calliper, a cloth and a file, even if I have to be discreet with the file. We are the little children of that production efficiency model known as Taylorism: our teachers promise us a beautiful future as qualified technicians, engineers even, at Peugeot in Sochaux. Filing metal to make a unique object is out of the question. No, it's quite the opposite. We must mass-produce on machines automated by our efforts. Expert inspection by highly qualified workers has now been replaced by an automated, binary and visual inspection system: a green light means the machined piece has the correct dimensions, a red light indicates that it does not meet the right specifications. 'Even our good Maghrebi friends who can't read or write can distinguish different colours,' one professor confidently declares. The Maghrebis are not permitted to have a file. Neither are we. If by chance you get caught using one, the sanction is immediate: you must cut out a piece of train rail with a metal saw, which is akin to using a spoon to drain out the sea. It will take you for ever.

I become well acquainted with the metal saw because, right from the outset, I hate the idea of becoming one of those white-overall wearers who will mistreat assembly-line workers. I apply all my incompetence and awkwardness. It comes easily to me because the moment I stride across the grey-tiled floor of the workshop, my legs begin to wobble. I particularly balk at having to use the lathe, a machine tool that sends me into a spin as much as the metal objects it machines. When I immobilise a part in the mandrel, I feel like a herdsman bringing a creature to slaughter. I can't even tune out as I watch the metal shavings come away, twirling in the cooling oil. I feel empty inside, telling myself what an idiot I have been. I am furious that I'm here instead of standing over a cooker at a secondary school doing catering studies. I can spend hours watching a bourguignon simmer, dreaming up new variations of my father's recipe, but boring a steel cylinder sends me into a complete torpor.

In any case I am not machining anything, I am just destroying. I acquire my reputation as the workshop dunce right from the earliest days. It's practically a game now between me and the teacher who instructs us in metal turning and milling, a former steelworker who has gained promotion through taking night-school classes. Unlike the other teachers, who only live for automated construction and who suggest I go and mow the school's front lawn, he has understood that I will always be on the wrong track, a system error between a milling and shaper machine. When he sees me losing the plot, he comes up and adjusts the machine so I don't break an instrument yet again. Whatever happens he will give me a ten out of twenty, so as to stop me from completely sinking. Sometimes I catch him sitting and reading at his desk. He has talked to me about Bernard Clavel, a writer who he says 'comes from these parts', and who he likes a lot. He lent me his novel, *La Maison des autres*, which is set in our town and depicts the life of an apprentice pastry chef. I had read out some of its passages to my father who replied: 'It's true, that's what it was like in the bakery.' The metal-turning teacher and I have this thing we do. At the end of the day he hands me the broom and, in a mock-haughty tone, exclaims: 'Right then, master sweeper, off you go!' I entertain myself making little heaps of dust till break-time. My schoolmates laugh as I bound around the place sweeping up the shavings.

We are a class of long-haired, bearded young males, who smoke strong tobacco roll-ups and sing Van Halen or Ange at the top of our voices. We burn rubber on two-wheeled machines, screeching around bends in a haze of pastis or beer. We conceal screwdrivers in the canteen mash to trigger strikes. We collect ball bearings as ammunition for the demonstrations we imagine ourselves going on. All of us, the milling-machine aces, the general class whizzes and the bulk of us less assured characters, are surprisingly good friends. I plumb the depths in technical classes, just about keep my head above water in science subjects, but come into my own in French, philosophy and history. We all stick together with a well-proven system of barter: I write essays and commentaries to swap for impeccable drawings of water pumps and gear trains.

In your kitchen you see me return each day from high school as if I'm a future graduate of the national conservatory of arts and crafts. I'm careful not to persuade you otherwise. Once out of the workshop, I'm immediately ecstatic at having escaped that godforsaken smell of metal. To remove the oil I furiously scrub my fingers with that soap whose gritty, sandlike texture leaves my fingers red. I like this act; I see myself as a worker, like you, not a lathe- or milling-machine operator. No, I'm just a working man washing his hands the way you do, your tea towel stuffed in your apron. I want to be a proletariat of nosh, a toiler over the ovens. I had told Gaby this one day when we were pruning a beech tree. He had said to me: 'Well, I'm not going to tell you otherwise but make sure you don't tell your father. He'll only get in a huff about it.'

And if that's your thing, consider me your future foreman when you're preparing those *oeufs en neige* . . .

I am convinced this misunderstanding will come to an end when I get this bloody baccalaureate. In the meantime I persevere with my drawing board. Every evening I begin with the worst, the intersection between a cylinder and a cone, and finish with the sweet nectar that is the novel *Sentimental Education*. For our French classes we have a tiny slip of a woman whose achievement is to make our horde of metalheads love Flaubert and Verlaine. Those wild beasts who stand on their Yamaha XL 125 motorbikes to hurtle down the steps of the Rue des Vieilles-Boucheries also dream of being adventurers in the vein of poets Blaise Cendrars and Arthur Rimbaud. They learn the pleasure of assembling words in the same minute detail as they make adjustments in the workshop.

At lunchtime on Saturdays I can finally swap my blue overalls for a commis chef's apron. My hands, so awkward when confronted with a drawing board and machine tools, finally know what they're doing. While you're grilling your skirt steaks with Lulu, I help you out with the chips. But above all I prepare my pâté de campagne for the next week. Every Saturday I replenish my range with pork jowl and belly, chicken liver, eggs and onions. I get on your nerves because I weigh the meat: 'Christ! Surely technical studies mean you can judge things by sight?'

Your mincer is probably the only mechanical object I could ever love. Every Saturday, once I've cleaned it, I put a little peanut oil into it, then cover it with a tea towel, its aroma one I will always love: the smell of fat, onions and spices together. I bolt it to the work surface and make sure the handle is properly positioned. I promise myself that one day I will draw it in Indian ink, so I can capture how a foundry managed to cast such an object, capture the magic of its volumes and hollows, its curves and straight lines. I would have liked to learn how to cast iron in sand instead of the merciless machine-tools I must make.

You watch me out of the corner of your eye as I trim the meat into strips. 'You can make them bigger, you know, you'll be there till this afternoon.' I pass them through the mincer with the onions. I mix in the eggs, salt, pepper and allspice. I like to knead raw food, hands steeped in meat and yolk. I love the glossy feel of the mix, the sting of an onion on a cut on my hand. I can't stop tasting it, adding a pinch of salt and a few twists of the pepper mill. I look at you for approval, but your look says: 'It's your pâté, you're in charge of what you're doing.' I line a large brown terrine with caul fat, that delicate white lace for covering pâté. When I place the terrine in the oven, you check there is enough water in the bottom of the bain-marie dish to cook it properly.

Today I'm also throwing myself into making beignets, which I have promised to take along to my first ever party on a Saturday night. You have said I can stay out till midnight. You clear away everything cluttering the work surface, then coat it with flour. The dough creates a fawn-coloured sheet when you spread it out. You stop to bellow: 'Where's the pastry cutter gone?' Lucien rummages around. He pulls out a mass of forks and spoons. The cutter cannot be found until you ask me to tip out the hotch-potch of whisks, ladles and spoons of every shape from a stoneware jar. Finally, from this disorder, a serrated cutter attached clumsily to a wooden handle emerges. You use this to make squares, triangles and circles in the dough. You throw a batch into the oil. The dough turns golden, you turn the beignets over in sequence as I continue cutting out more shapes for you.

I walk through the old town with a basketful of beignets wrapped in cloth under my arm. It's a cold dry night, the air smells of wood fires burning in chimneys. The music begins to get louder as I make my way along the little lane, passing under the imposing equine head at the horse butcher. You've always refused to cook with horse meat. You say horses look at you with human eyes when you take them to the slaughterhouse. I recognise Nina Hagen's voice from 'African Reggae' blaring out of a basement window. A flight of steps, a heavy door, then I am blinded by a strobe transforming the dancers' movements into a mass of disconnected limbs, thronging in a labyrinth of vaulted cellars. The air smells of damp, tobacco and patchouli. I'm rooted to the spot on the last step of the stairs with my basket of beignets. An arm yanks me towards my schoolmates, who encircle a bin filled with cans of beer. One of them cracks open a beer with his lighter and hands it to me. Another, by his side, opens a can with his teeth and drinks it in one go. We are like Apaches who have descended from the high plains of the housing estates onto a sweetshop of posh totty in the old town. This band of metal braves are perfumed with the pastis liberally imbibed before coming. Dressed in frayed army surplus jackets bought at American Stock, they look the youth dressed in Chevignon up and down. They laugh at the icing sugar that has brushed off onto my reefer jacket from the beignets, which they chew away on as they look scornfully at the 'pillocks' and 'slags' who study at normal secondary school.

One Apache takes things in hand: 'We could get them to try one of your doughnuts.' He makes a move on a brunette dancing alone. She is as surprised as if a bear had come up to offer her honey. She tries it and smiles. Soon the metal gang has turned into a saintly troupe surrounded by a sea of seraphic smiles. The class war will have to wait for another night. We cut loose to Deep Purple's 'Smoke on the Water', get closer during Led Zeppelin's 'Stairway to Heaven' and smooch to 'Hotel California'.

I am sitting on a staircase next to a grizzly bear, who is telling me about his first broken heart as he knocks back pastis as thick as custard. He rolls a wet joint which he struggles to puff on.

He tells me he 'likes me a lot', even if I am the laughing stock of the workshop. I can make out the church bell ringing 11 p.m. I tell myself that in an hour I will be in bed, I will have drunk three beers and will probably be suffering from extreme tinnitus because of the barrage of music from the speakers. All I can think about is my pâté. Before going to bed I might make a detour to the kitchen to try a bit around the edge. A tossing lion's mane appears in front of my eyes, which are blinded by the multicoloured lights. The mane falls away to reveal a pair of laughing green emerald eyes. She is called Corinne. She is the Grizzly's sister. She runs an affectionate hand through her now-slumbering brother's mop of hair. He is slumped over his lap, arms folded. She confesses that he has told her all about me, my essays and the chocolate truffles I make that everybody eats during maths lessons. I go red. Sting is singing, 'I'll Send an SOS to the World'. She wants me to dance with her. I stutter, 'I don't know how.' When she says, 'Don't worry, I'll teach you,' it's like a promise. I'm seventeen years old and I'm certain I've just met the love of my life.

I look at the clock of the bell tower. It's twenty to midnight. We are now sitting together under the awnings of the covered market. It's not that she's taken hold of my hand exactly, she has just gently entwined her fingers with mine. I dare not move. I hear thudding in my ribcage. I know she knows it's my first time. She blows her fringe away from her forehead and brings her face in close to mine. I have never kissed a girl. She takes charge. Her lips are as sweet as one of my doughnuts. I am floating over the clock tower. I'm scared to open my eyes. The bell chimes midnight. She pushes her moped vigorously to get it going and tells me over the sputtering: 'Tomorrow, three o'clock by the river.'

When I come into the kitchen my father is busy polishing his cooker. He points to a line drawn in chalk on the floor tiles. 'Close your eyes and follow it till you get to the wall.' With the focus of a tightrope walker, I step forward, keeping straight. My father stops me: 'Fine, you're not pissed.'

8

Corinne does not understand my Saturdays spent between the kitchen and my schoolmates. She can no longer tolerate sitting around on worn moleskin bar seats discussing motorbikes, Wilhelm Reich and Frank Zappa. Her hand squeezes mine under the table to say, 'Let's go.' The gang wink at me when we break away. On my bicycle, I hang onto Corinne's shoulder so she can tow me behind her moped. She lives in a villa in an upmarket housing development. I refuse to go through the front door to get to her bedroom. It's not that her parents would throw me out if they discovered me in their daughter's bed. In fact, they are very cool parents. I just like to play the alley cat, hoisting myself up the beams to the roof of the little farm adjoining her bedroom window. I know the David Hamilton photo over her bed by heart. Corinne is like the lavender scent of her duvet: reassuring and enveloping. Her family milieu emanates a kind of calm hitherto unknown to me. In my home my father, Nicole and Lucien love me, but it's a world of tobacco, pastis and the smell of cooking.

Corinne reaches for her alarm clock behind my shoulder. She is teasingly cursing because I've got to go back to my house at five in the morning. Every weekend she says the same thing, that we can have a lie-in at her house, we can do our home-work together and her parents will gladly have me for Sunday lunch. I just can't imagine leaving you on a Sunday, alone with the tick-tock of the clock and the smell of methylated spirits in the kitchen; the heavy silence made even more oppressive by the hum of the fridges.

Tonight Corinne was not at the Balto bar. I called her parents, but no one picked up. The week before, we had argued when she had pointed out to me that my hair smelt of chip fat. I replied to her that there was no shame in making chips, that chip fat was no worse than engine grease. She told me I was too sensitive, that she was only telling me for my own good. She kissed me, insisting that even if I smelt of cat's piss, she'd still love me. But I was already lost in my own thoughts. It was you they were getting at when they talked about my hair. I was proud to be the son of a prole who cherished his stove, who asked me to read out yet another article from *Tout l'Univers*. I felt jubilant watching you assemble your vol-au-vents with Lulu. I admired how you elegantly gutted and trussed a chicken. Try and explain that to a girl from a fancy neighbourhood, who can only see a pair of fingers up a chicken's arse. Try and explain how you made the most beautiful still life for me, with your casserole of cock's combs, kidneys and wild mushrooms. Try to convey the joy, each spring, of eating frogs cooked golden brown in butter and parsley, or the gamey, roasted scent of jugged hare.

I'm eighteen years old and my beautiful first love is breaking apart. My response is to zoom off down the road on a Yamaha XT 500 to Dijon. The rain is lashing my helmet, I am soaked to the bone, keeping my legs warm against the large four-stroke single-cylinder engine. My yellow headlights cut through the darkness, lighting up a display panel: Dijon 30 kilometres. I am going to Dijon. I know that Mum is there, has started her life over. I've often thought about it, taking a motorbike and going to see her. Today I am ready. I finally dare admit it: I miss her terribly.

I step on the throttle around an upward bend. My guts are steering me, not my brain, befuddled with one Picon beer too many at the Balto.

I have 'borrowed' the motorbike from a fellow Apache at school. I don't have a licence but enough alcohol in my blood to slump over the handlebars. On the roadside I see the neon light of a service station looming out of the darkness. I stop in its violently lit carpark. A German truck driver is about to draw the curtains of his cabin. He turns off his interior light. My feet squeak on the soaked gravel. I am cold.

I head into the service station. I barely have enough money in the pocket of my jeans to buy a coffee, and delude myself that I am sobering up. Dirty plates cover the counter. The boss is alone and grumpy. He puts my loose change in the till. I try to get interested in the wildlife documentary on the TV hanging in the corner by the bar. I know I won't make it to Dijon.

I pull up the collar of your old sheepskin jacket, which I still prefer to my reefer jacket. I wipe the wet seat of the motorbike with my handkerchief, get on and begin vigorously kickstarting it. When I lift up my head, a torch is lighting up my face. Two policemen are standing in front of me. They don't look hostile, just weary in the rain. I was not born under a lucky star when it comes to the cops. I don't have any of the motorbike's paperwork, don't have its registration documents or its insurance papers, because the bike belongs to a friend. I don't have any identity on me either. They make me get into their van. I still attempt to take charge of things: 'Yes, I've been drinking but not that much.' It's certainly enough to come up positive on the breath-alyser.

The police office smells of the carbon paper that will make a duplicate copy of my statement. Before starting to tap on his typewriter, one of the two policemen comments that I might be of age, but I've got all the maturity of an eight year old. I burst into tears when they ask for my father's telephone number. I try telling them that you've raised me alone, that you have enough problems already. The policeman leans back on his chair. 'You're still going to stay here with us a few hours, so you don't go home drunk.'

The sobering-up cell consists of a wooden bed frame and a hole in the ground with a flush chain worked from the outside. A radiator emits suffocating heat, which only reinforces the odour of shit and vomit. I am made to take off my belt and remove the laces from my shoes. I lie down and turn to face the wall. At this moment I could be in Corinne's arms, but I just want to tell the whole world to sod off. This isn't just adolescent belligerence, it's a rage that – to this day – still inhabits me once I've knocked back a bottle of Jack Daniel's or put my foot down in the fast lane. I want to shout from the rooftops about this inner loneliness that never goes away. I fall asleep humming Lou Reed's 'Lady Day'.

You're waiting for me in the police car park. The parents of the bike's owner have told you what's going on. I'm expecting a monumental beating. The kind that marks you for life.

You're staring at me, leaning against your car. Your blue eyes have never seemed so big to me, haunted by a mix of sorrow and hardness. I am waiting for you to unfold your arms and hit me. I want your anger, your reproaches, your insults and blows. I want anything but your immovable silence and that lead fucking lid that's been on your emotions ever since Mum left. I can't take the dark shroud of mourning that seems to envelop you, your soldiering monk's rectitude, sleeping by the stove. I don't want your lonely father courage, your emotionless transmission to me, our rituals floundering in the void. I want you to smash plates, to set fire to your kitchen, to get dead drunk on the floor with Lucien, your partner in death. I would like you to finally let go, to stop staring into oblivion while always expecting the worst. Your war is over, Dad. Give yourself permission to really beat the shit out of me. Memorably. Take a tooth out if you want. Hit me, spit in my face, but for God's sake say something instead of brushing another ghost under that carpet. Like you always do. I want you to give me the thrashing of my life.

You look at me from head to toe as if I'm a stranger. I am no longer anyone's son. You point for me to get in the car. Your movements are automatic as you drive along. You stop in front of the flower shop on the Grand-Rue. You hand me a fifty-franc note: 'Just say to her, "the usual".'

The florist sees me coming, shoots you a questioning glance. She assembles a bouquet of white roses with foliage. I clutch the bouquet. You keep driving, still in silence. We take an avenue that I know well. I've driven down it often to get to some terrain where we do motocross. Just before a hill lies the town cemetery. Two cypress trees frame its entrance, a harsh north wind blows through it. I've never known this place without that north wind blowing. Two paths bisect the cemetery in the shape of a cross. In front of me, you walk straight ahead. I shelter the roses under my arms from the wind. We come up to a square of grass planted simply with black crosses and the remains of some wilted flowers. Next to it are children's graves. I'm gulping cold air, my hangover and emotion are making my head spin. I stagger between two vaults, brush against a box tree, you hold me still. It's the beige marble shot through with red that I see first. My eyes follow up the stone until I get to the name and surname of a woman with two dates, one of which is my date of birth. I am hypnotised by the brilliance of the gold numbers and letters. You whisper to me: 'That is your mum, the one who brought you into this world. She died in childbirth.'

You place the rose bouquet on the grave. You take my hand. You kneel down and take out your knife and cut the flower stems. You put them in a vase filled with rainwater. You make a hole in the gravel and place the vase in it. You gently lean against the marble and hug it. I feel tears welling up. You put your hand on my shoulder.

'I met your biological . . . mother when I was an apprentice. She had been placed in the bakery to work as a salesgirl. We were both cut from the same cloth; neither of us had any family. She had been raised by nuns, I had been sent to a farm where I called the man and his wife "uncle" and "auntie". Very quickly, we started going out. We were wild kids, trusted no one, but we taught each other to love. On our day off we'd go to where I take you on Sundays. We had to be careful because our bosses wouldn't have liked it. On no account could they find out that the salesgirl was sleeping with the apprentice. She would have been sent back to the nuns sharpish, and I would have no doubt been sacked. Just the old baker knew. He fixed things by lending us his little place by the church. He would give us the key saying; "Go on, kids, these chances don't come around twice." When I was called up to Algeria, we decided to get married on my return. We wanted to have children. You came along quicker than expected. You were conceived while I was on leave. Your mother was about to give birth when I came back.'

'Why did she die?'

'They talked about a haemorrhage.'

'Why didn't I?'

'They did everything to save you, but she didn't make it.'

'The mother dies, the son lives. You call that *mektoub*, don't you?'

You swallow the saliva in your mouth and draw a cross in the gravel with your knife. I explode. 'You're full of shit. All these lies, yeah? You "discovered" the Relais Fleuri with Lucien, right? That's a load of crap!'

'It was your mother who found the Relais Fleuri. Personally, I was terrified at the idea of taking over a business, the clientele, the loans . . . but she was so full of life.'

'Why did you never tell me the truth?'

You sigh, search for your Gitanes cigarettes in your pocket. You light one and say those words that even today I can hardly believe you said: 'Forgive me.'

I walk the length and breadth of the tomb. I want to put my foot right down on a XT 500 and race everywhere around the graves. I turn around. You look pitiful, all hunched up, a little old man.

'And my Hélène, how does she fit in all this?'

'Hélène.'

You take a deep breath. 'Hélène was Hélène.'

'She's not dead at least, is she?'

'No.'

PART THREE

I

'And Dad, did he ever speak to you about my birth mother?'

Gaby does not appear all surprised by my question. 'Never.'

'And Hélène, did you know her?'

'A bit, but you know with your dad it's always been work-work-work, so it was hard to see them, to see all of you, together.'

As he smooths his roll-up, Gaby is looking at me out of the corner of his eye in a way that seems to say, 'Go on, kid, ask me some more questions.'

'What was she like, Hélène?'

'Beautiful, very beautiful. She had a spark in her, as they say. Imagine, a professor of letters like her. Although she never showed off her knowledge with us clods. Crazy about your dad as well.'

'And with me?'

Gaby pauses for a moment, weighing up his words: 'She was like a mother with her little boy.'

'So, why did she leave?'

'No one knows. Except your father.'

'Why has he never talked to me about it?'

'Because men don't talk about these things. Generally speaking. The only thing I know was that she said to your father: "You won't hear anything from me again."'

I jump up. With every ounce of my strength I smash my forehead against an oak tree. I stick my nails into the bark till they bleed. I swing around to find my knife. I want to slice it across my fists in one go, as if I am cutting off a chicken's feet. I see the roses on the marble of the tomb, Mummy Hélène's hair caressing my face when I come in to wake her. I see my father practically dropping from exhaustion as he polishes his kitchen in the silence of the night. I want to die. Gaby grabs the knife from me. I lunge for a piece of flint and smash my eyebrow with it. The blood runs. I see red, the dull liquid reaches my lips. Gaby grabs hold of my legs and tackles me to the ground. This man who has seen men emerging from tank turrets engulfed in flames; watched them die silently, ripped apart by rifle shot as they clutch at their entrails; men the colour of yellow or grey, left for days, dead and frozen under pea jackets like cardboard. A man who has seen every colour of blood, from bright red to black or garnet-coloured as it leaks on the snow, or on the butt of a gun or a soldier's puttees. He gets me to sit down with my head against his shoulder and pulls out his handkerchief to wipe my brow. I am crying. His wraps his hand around mine. It is warm and calloused.

'Why are you punishing yourself, kid? Don't you think you've had your fair share of hurt already?'

I shrug.

'You're not stupid. You're not clumsy, except in metal technology.'

He chuckles.

'Tomorrow you'll have your bac. You have your whole life ahead of you. And believe me, a life goes by quickly. Don't balls it up, son. Do what you want to do, not what others want. You just have to be a crafty bugger with your dad. You know he was on the receiving end of all this too. And with all this fuss, we haven't picked any wild garlic. We need to find some for dinner. Do you know how to poach eggs?'

Of course I know how to poach eggs.

After this I don't speak about my mother again. But I feel calmer. I revise for my exams at Gaby and Maria's house. Maria wakes me up at 5.30 every morning with a stroke of my cheek. 'Come on, gang, time to get up!' I hear her slippers shuffling to the cooker. It might well be May, but the mornings are chilly. She starts her fire. She fills the kettle. I open my eyes, roll over. I do my calculations: I have four weeks until my bac. It was Gaby's idea that I should come and revise at their house. Before I left, you and I had gone to put flowers in the cemetery. You rested your hand on my arm: 'I'm sure she watches over you.'

The kettle is whistling on the cooker, the smell of coffee fills the house. I get dressed, put on my Patauga boots, open the door to a frosty white morning. I walk around the house and go for a piss where I always do, facing the forest.

I aim my piss at a clump of dock leaves. A cat rubs up against my legs, returning after its night-time wander. Sometimes the cat comes back with a bird or mouse in its mouth. I sit down at the end of the table. Maria has put down a bowl of coffee, two pieces of toast, some butter and her jams. I contemplate my exercise books and pile of tomes at the other end of the table, a cat always in pride of place. I've also brought the first recipe book that I bought for myself: *Bocuse in Your Kitchen*. At the Relais Fleuri, it's kept hidden under my bed. I know your aversion towards anything that resembles a written recipe. In the evenings I immerse myself in mackerel with white wine vinegar, poached eggs in Beaujolais and chocolate and vanilla marble cake. The book must be kept fully in view on the table in Gaby and

Maria's house, in case I spend more time revising the recipe for hot *saucisson* instead of the probabilities and processes of machining. I try my hardest to go over lessons that I don't understand at all, in the hope that I don't get a question on them come exam day. I am unbeatable on Béchamel but incapable of explaining 'broaching'.

After drinking his coffee in bed with Maria, Gaby sits himself down opposite me to have his breakfast. He has compiled a time-table of near-military precision for me. I revise hard from 6 a.m. till 10 a.m. in the morning then from 1 p.m. till 4 p.m., with another hour after dinner. Between these periods of revision, I trail around after Gaby and am allowed to go into the kitchen. Yesterday afternoon we killed a rabbit. I've never met anyone slaughter a little creature like he does. He is methodical and affec-tionate at the same time. When he gets the rabbit out of the hutch, he caresses it and whispers its name. All of them have been baptised. This one is called Trotsky. There is also a cockerel called Bakunin and a duck called Jaurès. The frying pan is the equivalent of the Panthéon mausoleum for these great animals. 'Life with us was not bad, was it? Grass and good hay, and what about those bowls of winter vegetable mash?' he lists as he takes the small ash log from his jacket to knock out Trotsky. He hangs the rabbit up by its two back feet and lets it bleed out. As a thin stream of blood drains into the bowl Gabriel often likes to repeat, 'In the end, we're all insignificant.' After he has skinned the rabbit, he lays it on a plate and covers it with a cloth and solemnly says, 'Here lies Comrade Trotsky,' before taking the rabbit to Maria. She lets out a little gasp. She tells him off in Russian. He takes her by that slender waist of hers and showers her in kisses. Maria also speaks Russian when they make love. When I asked Gaby in the forest why they didn't have any children, he stopped sharpening the chain of his saw: 'Because of everything Maria endured.' I trembled at the anger as he pulled the chainsaw's starter.

Maria gazes lovingly at me. 'Do you want me to help you?'

I tell her no. I am preparing a bouquet garni with a bay leaf, thyme, the white bulb of a leek and a sprig of lovage. I cut a beautiful thick slice of bacon.

'Have you got a chopper, Maria?'

'A what?' she replies, taken by surprise.

Gabriel is laughing his head off:

'You know, a chopper, do you think you've got one?'

Maria realises that we are winding her up. 'Piss off,' she retorts.

Gaby gets out a curved cleaver with a handle either side. He mimics a chopping action. 'This is what you call a herb chopper.'

Maria pretends to tell us off: 'You can't just say a cleaver, can you? You French, you always have to complicate things.'

Gabriel slides the blade over a sharpening stone several times. He always says: 'In whatever job, a good worker is someone who knows how to keep their tools sharp.' In his 4L there is a beautiful American World War II folding shovel that he keeps as sharp as a blade. I've read somewhere they were used in hand-to-hand combat during the war.

On the cutting board I chop up the rabbit's liver, lungs and heart with some parsley and garlic. I mix it all up in a bowl with a little glass of Gaby's moonshine. It tastes of the almond-flavoured stones of the plums that we go and pick after the first frosts. As for those buckets of blue plums, you need quite a few of those to make a litre of eau de vie. Gaby distils everything that grows around him: apples, pears, elderflowers and morello cherries. Each morning he drinks his 'drop', as he calls it, poured into the warm bottom of the cup of his second coffee. He also makes his own vinegar with the remains of old wine. I pour a dash of it into the bowl of fresh rabbit's blood . . . Gaby comes up and pokes me with his elbow as I'm stirring the meat.

'Will this do you?' he says, showing me a dusty bottle.

'It's an Aloxe-Corton Premier Cru 1972.'

'Don't you think it's a bit much for jugged hare?'

Gaby whispers in my ear: 'I'm setting the bar high; you'd better not cock it up.'

I put the wine on the heat. I sprinkle the rabbit pieces with flour, coating them. I add some hot water to bind it all together. I pour in the boiling wine, add the bouquet garni and unpeeled garlic cloves. I place the casserole dish on a corner of the stove so it can simmer slowly. 'Not there, it will cook too quickly', Maria suggests. She is like you, she knows the different heats of her stove by heart. The times you made me feel the stove's iron for the best spot for boiling or, conversely, to cook on a very low heat . . .

In the village everyone knows that Lulu likes men. When Gaby came back from the war, he found out his father had hit him when he had been caught with another lad in the woods. Their mother had pleaded with Gaby not to say anything to his father, who was pulling out potato plants in his garden. Gaby squared up to him, his gaze now that of a soldier's.

'Lucien is my brother. If you ever raise a hand to him again, you'll deal with me. You may be my father, but I will smash your face in.' The old man's eyes clouded over. He feared this son, whom the war had emboldened to speak freely and with authority. 'There's still a queer living under my roof,' he had whispered.

'So what? Would you have liked him to end up in Auschwitz?' The father looked down at his potato plants.

I take out the rabbit meat from the casserole dish, strain the sauce, then put it back on the heat before adding the mix of liver, lung and heart. I stir it carefully, assessing the sauce's texture. Gaby dips some bread into it, his eyes half-closed in pleasure as he tastes it. 'Like Jesus wearing velvet underpants!' he announces.

I can hear you saying: 'Sauce chef: that's the best job in the kitchen.' I knew magic was happening when, as a child, I watched you making your crayfish bisque. The creatures turned bright red in the casserole pot while I busted a gut making the mirepoix of vegetables for you to add. You would furiously crush the lot using a rolling pin like a pestle – the tomatoes, white wine, cloves, juniper berries and black peppercorns – all to add colour to the mix. Afterwards you would leave it to cook for three hours on a low heat, forgotten on the corner of your stove. The bisque turned into a thick sauce that you'd filter through a strainer. You had to add cream, of course. You made me taste this sorcery. Today I'm just as proud of my rabbit dish when I see Gaby and Maria's satisfaction. I know if I call to tell you, you will immediately start asking me about how my revision is going. In our home we don't reheat arguments, we bury them. I've absorbed this to such an extent that I am caught completely off guard when my form teacher asks me what I plan to do after my exams. I have forbidden myself from talking about cooking, scared you would hear about it. The idea of engineering school is also out of the question, given my uselessness at technical subjects. I feel so disarmed, I opt for ultimate provocation: 'I'll do anything – just nothing that I've tried to learn here.' My schoolmates fall about laughing at their desks.

If I had repeated this scene to you, you would have got on your high horse and said again and again, 'You can't do that.' Gaby, on the other hand, he told me I had panache. When I revise, he likes browsing through my schoolbooks, a cat snuggled up to him. Although he doesn't know a thing about chemistry he makes me recite the definitions. Mind you, he is much better than me at mechanical engineering, without having ever studied it. Just by reading a plan he can picture the workings of a clutch.

'This is actually all quite simple,' he says, 'a matter of common sense.' When he can see I am about to get into a muddle, he tells me to 'give it a break now' and to go out and get some air. He makes me put on boots because we are going across the nearby muddy marshes, known as the *gouilla*, to pick wild garlic.

This afternoon the sky opens up to let out short bursts of rain. Between these downpours large clouds gather like sheep in the blue of its expanse. Gaby has parked his 4L in a former sand quarry bordered by broom. We walk around the bushes through a copse of birch and beech trees. Gaby has never liked a beaten path. He takes me to the middle of nowhere, on paths where he manages to never get lost. We walk through a vast clearing followed by a succession of steep, narrow valleys where the water comes up through the earth under dead leaves. Gaby stops on a heather-covered cliff overlooking a small valley where little streams interweave. We step across them, jumping on clumps of buttercups and piles of pebbles. I am bold enough to ask him, 'You know where we're going, right?' Gaby keeps walking, doesn't turn around as he replies: 'What do you think?' We walk along the side of an ever-swelling stream when we catch sight of the green of a pasture by the forest. Gaby lowers a barbed-wire fence so I can step over it. We walk through the lush grass. You couldn't really call it a prairie, despite the presence of some heifers, which move away when they see us. It isn't a glade either, even though clustering tall oak trunks soar up around us. We head towards a barn standing in the shade of these great trees. It has fallen into ruin. A part of the roof has collapsed onto what looks like its hayloft. We sit on a stone lintel, carved with the numbers '1802'.

'That's the date of construction,' Gaby explains.

'And the date of Victor Hugo's birth,' I add.

He taps me on the shoulder: 'An anarchist like us, right?'

'Blimey, you really have to know your way around to get here.'

'A bit, but that's what I like. It turned out to be very useful to us in the war, this barn. The Resistance used it as a meeting place.'

'Wasn't it watched over by the Germans?'

'Not that much. We always had guys come and scout it, to check the place was safe whenever we needed to meet up. And, by the end, the Germans had so much to deal with in the towns, they didn't bother turning up here.'

I carve a piece of hazel that I plant in the ground like an arrow.

'Hey, I'd say you prefer carving wood to machining iron.'

I laugh. Gaby keeps his eyes on me, pensive, as I strip the bark of a second branch. 'Do you still want to be a cook?'

My expression makes it clear.

'You'd have to go to cookery school, even with everything you already know.'

'I need to perfect my skills. I could do it in a school or working at someone's restaurant. But it will always cause the same old fuss with my dad.'

Gaby concentrates as he rolls a cigarette. 'Have you asked him?'

'No, but I know.'

'Kid, you've got to be crafty with your dad. After you get your bac, don't rub him up the wrong way. Enrol yourself somewhere to go through the motions, make him believe that one day you'll be a teacher. And then find yourself a good boss to learn more about cooking your grub. You'll see, it will all work out.'

Something happened that day on those rocks warmed by the spring. It was as if this wily old fox of a man was setting me on the right course. Together we had talked more that afternoon than I ever had with my father on the Sundays spent by the river in my childhood. From my fingers Gaby takes the cigarette that I'm struggling to roll. 'What do you call that, a joint? Hand it over here.'

2

You prove to be the most generous of fathers when all my mates show up at the restaurant to celebrate their results. I change the draught beer cask, which empties in the blink of an eye. I fill rows and rows of glasses with the slightly fizzy, white wine-based aperitif, Blanc Limé, synonymous with celebration. You decide to fill your big two-handled casserole with potatoes cooked in their skin and served with every cheese that we have in the larder. We drink, eat, gorge ourselves, flirt, throw up and drink again. And you, you work flat out in the kitchen, a Gitane burning on the edge of the cooker. You decorate servings of sorbet with your almond tuile biscuits. Lulu, who has just got himself a large glass of iced water from the bar, says to me: 'Your father has gone mad, I've never seen him like this.' We drink to the health of the Relais Fleuri all the way out to the forecourt of the station, railway staff included. Even the teachers and local police are here: you've opened the champagne for them.

Corinne is sitting at a table on the terrace with a group who, like her, have all passed with distinctions. After the holidays she'll go and study advanced mathematics at the Lycée du Parc in Lyon. I offer her – and the school friends with whom she is chatting – a glass of champagne. I am playing my role of restaurant boy to the gilded youth. I am enjoying it. As Gaby said when I was with Corinne, I was punching, big time. I look at her as if she is a delicate porcelain doll, wondering how my worker's hands could have ever touched her. I discover that love can tiptoe out of your heart without breaking it.

I'm also discovering that a man's brain is his second sexual organ. Corinne looks up: 'What are you going to do after the summer?' I'm pretty tanked up on Picon beer and I'm necking a bottle of champagne. I want to be silly. My mate Bébert walks by; he's also pissed as a newt on Ricard. Like a few of the others, he's off to study at the prestigious École Polytechnique, but that won't stop him shaving around bends on his XT 500 or eating Henaff pâté straight from the tin with me at three in the morning. We snog each other and shout: 'We are going to get married and have a baby!'

In fact, it must be 3 a.m. Even the geraniums on the terrace are tired. Yet the Relais Fleuri will not empty. You drink a beer at the door. Your eyes look over the terrace. You smile as you watch the young ones, all snogging each other now. I think you are happy. You clap your hands: 'Right, time to get stuck into the onion soup.' I want to help you but you say, 'No, stay with your friends.' I hate you.

You won't have me in your kitchen any more. As far as you're concerned, I've got my qualification and I've made it to the other side. I'm practically a white-collar worker now. It's all over: the commis chef's blue apron, the buckets of potatoes to peel, the smell of Morteau sausage and garlic on my fingers. And over, too, is the khaki rucksack from American Stock to take to school, because you've managed to buy me a briefcase and tasselled loafers to replace my Clarks scribbled with biro. I want to piss you off one more time before I embark on this bourgeois life you've imagined for me. I nick the keys of Bébert's motorbike. I kick-start it viciously and rev its single-cylinder engine. I'm about to get into first gear when an unbelievably powerful fist grabs me by the neck and cuts the engine. I recognise Lucien's long, gnarled fingers. He plants himself in front of the handlebars and stares at me with his big sad eyes. 'Enough, Julien.'

The next day we look like death and consume litres of Coca-Cola to subdue our hangovers. We must clear out our lockers. We have planned to burn our blue overalls in an almighty barbecue by the river. I struggle to open the door of my locker, bent from too much use. I put my calliper, spanners and file in my saddlebag. I run my hand over the top shelf. There is a sealed envelope. In it I find a folded piece of paper. I open it. Someone has written 'Hélène' in capital letters, with a phone number. I read the name and number over and over again. I have an appalling headache. I count the digits and there's no mistaking it, it's a phone number. Panic overwhelms me; I am frightened I will lose the number. I immediately write down the digits in my essay book. I stand in a daze as all around me the metal-head gang sing and vigorously kick their lockers. They bash me with a rumpled porn magazine and give me a hard time when I chuck it in the bin. Clearly I don't mix well with hangovers, they tell me.

I walk back down the avenue. A phone box stands at the bottom of the hill, beyond an advertising hoarding. The gardener that I regularly walk past is weeding his strawberry patch. He turns to look at me. Does he know this will be the last time we see each other? For a brief moment I feel like saying goodbye to him, but cannot pull myself away from the damn telephone box, its open door an invitation. I have a one-franc piece. I turn it over and over in my trouser pocket as I walk; I take it out to be sure it is one. I reread the number. I don't know what to do.

I'm terrified at the thought of hearing her voice, which I can no longer remember. She left nearly ten years ago. Without saying a word to me. Ten years since the light went out. To not call her is to have no hope of ever understanding why. To call her means knocking on the door of a stranger who wiped my face, dressed me, fed me, cuddled me, and then disappeared. I am pierced with remorse. I retrace my footsteps. I can see the gardener under the hoarding; he straightens up and observes me. Have I become so strange looking? I pick up the receiver; it smells of bad breath and stale tobacco. I take a deep breath but my fingers lose themselves in the numbers as I dial. I put the phone back down. I stroke a heart engraved on the metal of the box. I pick the receiver up again but my heart is beating too hard. The one-franc piece rolls out of the slot. I stare at it in the crook of my hand. You can't cheat *mektoub*. Heads, I call her, tails, I don't. I throw the coin right up in the air. It falls back down onto the gravel. It's tails. I can't stop here though. I need a moment of magic. I toss it one more time, now it falls heads up. One-all and into extra-time. I shake the coin in a closed fist and make it roll like a dice. Tails. *Mektoub* has decided it for today. I will not call her.

On Sunday we go to celebrate my results with lunch at Maria and Gaby's house. I am sitting in the car with your strawberry cream cake on my lap and your casserole of *coq au vin* between my ankles. This is the second time I have seen you in a white shirt, ever since the parent–teacher meeting in Year 10. As we drive through the forest you tell me about fern shoots that can be eaten like asparagus. I am on the verge of asking you: 'Can we try finding them?' but change my mind. I've often bitten my tongue on making plans, for fear they won't materialise. This isn't about superstition, though. I can't imagine a future between us knowing that – for you – cooking will never be part of it.

Gaby and Maria have already started on the aperitifs. They are sniggering: 'So, Mr Baccalaureate, do you still want to talk to us?' I hate their fooling around. Gaby adds: 'You know what he says, that Bocuse: I've got two bacs. One in the front and one in the bac!'

Maria takes hold of my face and kisses me noisily. I can feel her tears. Gaby and Lucien's mother is there. 'My congratulations,' she says.

This little wrinkled apple of a woman has lived through two wars, scraped to make ends meet to feed two nippers, but still she addresses me with that formal 'vous' that I cannot stand. I gulp down the Pontarlier that Gaby has given me in three mouthfuls. I feel nauseatingly numb. I drink a second, then a third. No one says a thing. I am the hero of the celebration. I am in an alcoholic haze, muffled voices come at me, along with a never-ending succession of hands patting my shoulder: 'Who's a clever boy then!' 'The first baccalaureate in the family!' 'You won't talk to us now you're part of the elite . . .' Maria has saved the biggest and best of her morel mushrooms for me, served in cream. You select the finest bits of your coq au vin to give to me. My glass is never empty. Gaby has uncorked a Romanée-Conti from my year of birth, tracked down by his network of former Resistance members. In the midst of all this hubbub, I am forever trying to catch his eye. He knows this, has fun with it. When I manage to catch his gaze, his eyes are laughing, as if to say: 'So, kid, a child prodigy are you? Don't blow it, all right? Do as we agreed.'

You cut your strawberry cream cake, Gaby cracks open a bottle of champagne. We drink a toast. The cold and the bubbles perk me up. Gaby throws me a lifeline: 'What are you going to do now?' All eyes are on me: 'Literature studies.' I am surprised by my calm voice. You push a strawberry around your plate. You try very hard to say solemnly, 'That's good, son,' but it's not enough to mask your disappointment as you cut more slices of your cake. You want me to be an engineer in an office. I could have designed the TGV or Concorde, or even the new Peugeot. How proudly you'd be telling your diners: 'My son is an engineer at Sochaux.' Instead here I am about to dive into a world of books and, who knows, I might end up as a literature teacher like Hélène. You are too thick-skinned for me to tell whether you think about her or not, but I am convinced she still inhabits you. What I don't tell you is that I plan to get taken on in a kitchen.

Along with Gaby and Lucien you toast me with some eau de vie and force a few laughs. I go and lie in the field at the front of the house. Ever since I discovered it in my locker, Hélène's telephone number has haunted me. I've written it out on yet another piece of paper, which I take out of my trousers. My head spins with possible scenarios. Imagine if she picks up? Should I say first, 'Is this Hélène's house?' or just, 'It's me, Julien.' 'Hello Hélène,' or 'Hello Mum?' And what if she hangs up immediately after recognising my voice or says, 'I'm sorry, you've got the wrong number'? Or there might just be a long silence because I don't dare speak. She might say: 'Julien, I've waited so long for your call.' Again I would go blank and she would sigh loudly and ask: 'What have you been up to?' No, I don't want her to talk to me like that. 'What have you been up to?' is what people say when they are only pretending to be interested. We might not have anything to say to each other. I would apologise politely and run out of the phone box.

3

It feels like I've been sitting in the post office for a lifetime. I am combing through the phone book identifying numbers that end in '60' like Hélène's. As I am still undecided about calling her, I am attempting to locate her, in the hope she is not ex-directory. Next door the school bell rings. At midday the post office will close. The post office clerk has watched me hunched over the phone book all morning and approaches me.

'Are you learning it by heart?'

I turn crimson and mumble, 'No, I'm looking for somebody's number.'

The clerk gives me a knowing look. 'Can I see the numbers you have in your hand?'

I hand him my piece of paper. He smiles. 'No point looking in the Côte-d'Or. Your number is in the Doubs, probably Besançon.'

There I had been, imagining myself setting off to Dijon in search of Hélène, and here I am now, poring over Besançon numbers. I had no idea that I could be so patient. I finally come across the address that matches the number. It's not her surname, the first name belongs to a man. It's like a punch in the stomach. She has got married, probably even had children, while time stood still in our house after she left. My father never started over and my biological mother, she didn't ask to die. Hélène betrayed us. I feel angry at this posh bitch who thought she knew better than everyone else, who never had to put her hands in the grease. I feel contempt for her. But I'll be the one to study literature. I didn't need to be born with a silver spoon in my mouth. I'll go to college in the M43 jacket that Gaby gave me, not some Burberry raincoat.

You seem pathetic to me when I find you in the kitchen. Suddenly everything looks shabby. The paper napkins in the restaurant, the smell of pastis and Gauloises, your tired old stews, Lucien's shuffling step, the shower next to the kitchen, the shambles upstairs and Nicole's dyed hair – Nicole, who has dressed like a crow ever since André died in a car crash. And all this time Hélène must have been living her worthy, comfortable life in Besançon, her kids in checked Bermuda shorts, Alice bands and Peter Pan collars, bridge on Sundays, Rotary Club bring-and-buys, skiing in Switzerland in the winter, Côte d'Azur in the summer . . . You interrupt the movie in my head: 'Have you enrolled at Dijon yet? Don't you think it's about time?'

'No. I'm enrolling at Besançon.'

I say it without thinking. It is as if I have always lived in that town without ever setting foot in it. The name feels familiar to me when I say it, even though I only know it from images on regional TV. I can see its dark streets, the old stones, and I can imagine myself in an attic under the roof, piles of books my only furniture, a plank of wood on two trestles for a desk and a mattress on a bit of old, worn carpet. As for you, you're not at all surprised by my reply. Dijon, Besançon, it's all the same to you, a half-hour train ride. Though you do ask me: 'Why Besançon?'

I make myself sound superior: 'Because it's Victor Hugo's birthplace.'

You defer to my knowledge. I hate you when you doff your cap to me like this. I try and convince myself that Besançon is not because of Hélène. I only want to understand what happened, then I'll leave her be. Buying a map of the town at the bookshop, I set myself out a plan for the next few days. I will enrol at the literature faculty, find a room to stay, start my classes, and only then will I go and see where she lives.

I'm on the railcar. And, like any adventurer rolling into an unknown town, I'm smoking Ajja 17 tobacco. Next to me is my rucksack, which you have filled with the minutiae of your former soldier's life. My sleeping bag, towels and sheets, a toilet bag and enough provisions to survive a siege: *saucisson*, fruit, plain biscuits, two tins of Olida pâté and a lemon cake. You've given me endless bits of advice along with two signed cheques and some cash. You've suggested that I roll some notes up in a sock because 'you never know what might happen'. You have made me promise that I will go and stay in the hotel that you've called to book for me. I wonder how an ex-sergeant from the Algerian Jebel, celebrated by Lucien, could have turned into such a mother hen.

Stepping outside the Gare de Viotte station, Besançon is nothing like I had imagined. It's a green town nestled between hills and the meanderings of the Doubs river. I walk down the Rue Battant in the cold air of an autumn day. It takes just a few strides for me to immediately adopt this colourful, working-class neighbourhood as my own. The world hails you bright and early here among the couscous restaurants, bars and artisans' studios. I sit down on the terrace of a café. Everything seems wonderful to me. The coffee served in a little glass, the smell of grilled chicken, the grey of the ancient stones In a wave of enthusiasm

I ask the café owner if he knows of a room to rent. My question does the rounds of the counter, the surrounding houses and along the whole street. A man comes up to me, offering me an elbow by way of greeting because his hand is covered in white paint. He has a room to rent on the top floor, above his studio. I can go and see it if I want. I'm a bit overwhelmed by the speed of events, but also by how easy things can be in life. I decide to go. A beautiful staircase, narrowing as it rises, leads to a room on the sixth floor. The landlord, who behaves instantly as if we're old acquaintances, explains to me that he is a carpenter. 'You'll see, it's simple but clean.' The room is past a bend at the end of a corridor, by the toilets. It looks like the end of the boat's passageway in the film *The Drummer-Crab* that I went to see at the MJC cinema.

There is just enough space for a bed, at the end of which a table is wedged against the wall. You have to step over the chair to get into the room. A sink and a wardrobe complete the furnishings. Through the transom window a ray of light dapples the floral bedspread. The place smells nicely of polish. In my mind I see myself retracing my footsteps from this little roost down to the street. I feel free and solitary here. The landlord doesn't want a cheque, he is happy to do without a deposit if I pay him in cash. I pay the rent with my notes. Here I am at home already! I get up on the bed to look at a sea of old roof tiles from the window. Some crows are cawing on a chimney. I race down the road all the way to the bridge, the Pont Battant, where I find the brown waters of the Doubs. I stroll along the quays up to the Parc Chamars. I sit under some trees to cut a piece of sausage. I have never eaten alone like this, propped against the trunk of a tree, the hum of cars in the distance. I don't give Hélène a moment's thought in these surroundings, although they must be familiar to her. I embrace the town while munching biscuits.

In the afternoon I enrol in literature classes at the Rue Megevand. The place smells of old books and waxed wooden floors. I have a copy of my bac certificate in my pocket and a black biro to fill in the forms. I feel even more of a lone grenadier-skirmisher, boosted by two beers at the university bar. In the evening I give up a whole five-franc piece to call you. Yes, I am now a student; yes, I'm sleeping at the hotel because it hasn't been easy to find a room, you see . . . meaning, I don't know when I'm going to be back. I can sense your disappointment. One more time you tell me not to leave any money hanging around the room 'because you can't be sure of anyone'. I laugh as I hang up.

I'm one of the last few to arrive in the lecture theatre. I get vertigo at the top of the stairs. I sit at the back, at the end of the row. It is mainly girls. I am surprised at this, a bloke who has just left a gang of rugged metal-workers. Some have mani-cured nails. It all seems very refined to me. The lecturer is red-haired, dressed in a suit and tie. He says hello to us as if we were only just chatting the day before. He opens a red leather briefcase and starts to read out his lesson. It is about Corneille's *Le Cid*. I don't understand a word of what he says in his self-important tone; his sentences are swallowed up by an intolerable lisp. I am unable to take down any of it in note form. I envy the tall guy with brown hair in front of me who is filling pages with black ink. To my left, two girls are whispering and laughing. One of them is stroking her hair to show what she thinks is the professor's toupee. I ask myself what the hell I am doing here. I imagine the big trees in the Parc Chamars losing their leaves, the autumn mushrooms. I see myself standing with Gaby under a bower, the arch of some hazel trees. He would tell me that he is happy I have chosen Besançon because it's the capital of Charles Fourier and his utopian socialism. He would tell me the story of the clockmakers' strike in 1973, the fights of Jean Josselin, the working-class boxer from Besançon and French and European welterweight champion in the 1960s; how he failed in his bid for the world title in 1966 in Dallas. We would uncover a golden carpet of girolles. Maria would come and sit on 'her man's knee'. I would feel desire.

I wander through the university canteen with my tray. I don't dare sit with the other students. I walk around for a good while before I find an empty table. I feel sick from the smell of bleach and ready-made stock. The mash is cold, the meat stringy and the sauce has a burnt bone flavour. I eat my dry bread and a banana. From this moment on, I always go back to my little roost to eat, feeding myself almost exclusively on barley bread rolls from the Arab corner shop on the Rue Battant. I dip them into beautiful, dark olive oil. I will also devour slices of bread with harissa because nothing works better than chilli if you are feeling low. I also dig at a bowl of almonds that I keep on my desk, as I try to decipher the meaning of *Le Cid*. I feel like I am learning a foreign language with Corneille. I cannot find meanings or feelings in any of his words. If they could see me now, my metal mates would say that I was 'farting around over nothing'.

One afternoon in October a tall beanpole of a man with an aquiline nose and a black cape showed up in our lecture theatre. He took his shock of frizzy hair for a walk around the rows. He sat on his desk without notes and held us rapt for two hours. He said that the university was crazy to produce graduates only capable of regurgitating tutors' lessons. He warned us that with him it would be unthinkable to follow rules in the same way; we were here to take an apprenticeship in freedom of thought and writing. I was blown away. It reassured me to know that Gaby thought in the same way and – in another life – this man could have been him, a professor of comparative literature. I kept his reading list for the year in my cookery book, *Bocuse in Your Kitchen: A Midsummer Night's Dream*, Huysmans's *À Rebours*, some Romantic German texts and Fassbinder. He is the only one of our professors who doesn't recommend that we read his books. I compare him to you: neither a recipe book or a handout, just eyes and ears to follow you, Ariadne's thread.

On All Saints' Day I resolve to do it. It's a frosty day. I am drinking coffee downstairs. The couscous simmering in the kitchen creates condensation on the windowpane. The owner offers me some almonds and dates because I have a bad cold. The old radiator at the end of my bed has packed up. I had to sleep wearing all my jumpers. I had promised you that I would come back on 1 November but I keep pushing back the date. My life changed when I got onto that railcar. On the phone I swapped my five-franc piece for a one because I had so little to say to you. Even if I still have some change, I leave him high and dry when the line cuts off and interrupts his irritating questions. Was I eating? Wasn't I cold? Was what I was learning difficult? I want to shout at him, 'Leave me alone, you're not my mother.'

A sombrely dressed group are going to All Saints' Day mass at Sainte-Madeleine. I cross the Doubs river, swollen with autumn rain. I scrabble in my pockets to find enough to buy myself a packet of tobacco. I don't need a map to guide me. I know her street, even if I have stopped myself till now from passing by it. I film her neighbourhood in my mind: the baker, the butcher, the florist where she probably goes, the newsagent's where maybe she still buys *Le Monde* and her Royale menthols. I walk along shiny paving stones, imagining the brown riding boots first, then the beige coat and scarf that set off the dark, lively mass of her hair. The closer I get to the even numbers of her street, the more I hug the walls. I am frightened of bumping into her. I stick close to the large arched entrances so I can hide if she appears.

At her address I find a closed front entrance and high walls overrun with Virginia creeper. I stand back to take the measure of the façade, deciding it must be one of those private town mansions tucked away in old Besançon. I attempt to push open the door but it's locked. On the door frame I find a row of bronze doorbells, one of which has the name from the phone book. My hand hovers over the bell even though I know I will not press it. I decide to take a walk around the neighbourhood. I sit on the bandstand stairs in the Place Granvelle. The sun illuminates the bare trees in pale light. From my pocket, I take out *Strayings of the Heart and Mind* by Crébillon fils and I try to read it. As ever, superstition dictates that I must read ten pages before I can return to her front entrance. A child's voice makes me jump. What if she takes her own child walking here? I run and hide behind the trunk of a tree. A little girl walks by followed by a young blonde woman. The church bell strikes eleven. I finish a chapter of Crébillon. I clench my fists in my pockets and stride purposefully back. The now open entrance looks onto a paved courtyard decorated with trimmed box trees in pots. High windows run across the three façades of the mansion; a German saloon car is parked by the front door.

In a mix of fury and apprehension I walk into the courtyard. I am the para in *The Longest Day* descending on Normandy,

6 June 1944. I can only come out of this a victor or a loser. I position myself right in the middle of the courtyard. I could shout out, then I think to myself that the hand of *mektoub* is at play.

I look at the beautifully carved oak door and I imagine it opens. Hélène puts her head around the door and widens her eyes: 'Is that you, Julien?' She smiles at me and says: 'Come.' I do not move. She walks towards me, I recognise her perfume, she takes me in her arms. Victory. Defeat is a half-open door, her voice or some unknown one saying: 'Who do you want, young man?' Shit scared, I mumble a lie and turn away on my heels.

The bell strikes midday. I study the windows and curtains. No movement. Not even the sound of footsteps or the echoes of a voice coming down the staircase. I retrace my steps and take up a position on the corner of the street. I hear the engine of the saloon and doors slamming. I make out the driver, a man with a thin face and gold-rimmed glasses. I can see a figure next to him, the flame of a lighter, two children in tow. I walk away. Neither victory nor defeat.

4

There's 'foie gras, green beans' for a group of four. I meticulously arrange the beans on the plate, I add parsley leaves and put down the plate in front of the second in command who is pan-frying the foie gras. I return to my station to prepare radishes when I am shoved in the back. The second is holding the plate out to me. He has a tuft of hair under his nose that gives him an arrogant air. 'Is this how they taught you to trim beans?' My hands freeze in the icy water where I am washing the radishes. Another shove: 'We're not in your greasy spoon for country bumpkins; we're *cooking* here, not feeding calves.' The contents of the plate are hurled into the dustbin. He spells it out, right up to my ear: 'With beans, you trim them length-wise, quickly, otherwise I'll smash your face in.' I pull the cutting board towards me and, one by one, I go through a clutch of green beans. I hear the second muttering to the chef: 'Comes from the arse-end of nowhere and wants to play with the big boys.'

The chef says nothing. His mind is elsewhere, as usual. When he took me on as an occasional extra, he just asked me, 'Are you sure you want to work in this profession?' I hid the fact I was a student. I was intimidated by the décor, the red velvet seats, the dark panelling, the marble and multitude of mirrors.

He proffered a limp hand; the interview bored him. He wasn't looking at me, he was watching the room being set up. It was the first time I had ever seen a waiter iron a tablecloth on a table. Another was polishing the cutlery with white vinegar. The chef looked at his nails as he talked to me about nouvelle cuisine, lighter sauces, minute cooking times and vegetables on the plate as found in the garden.

The Gault & Millau guide is the only thing he can talk about. It had given him a wonderful review the year before. Michelin is a whole other game, the chef's silent obsession and a taboo subject in the kitchen. Since the first moment he began waiting for that star, the chef has dreaded and loathed the 'red guide' in equal measure. All it takes is a diner with a serious look to create a major commotion in the kitchen. The chef must see and check everything. He will be the one to arrange the amuse-bouches on the plate and pile questions on the maître d' who must keep vigil over the VIP table.

Did the man study the menu at length? Did he ask for explanations? Did he pause between courses? Why did he take the market menu and not the gourmand menu? Did they explain the wine menu to him? Which one did he order a glass of? Sometimes the chef watches the intruder beadily from a hidden corner of the bar. He thinks that he's seen him before. Or maybe not. He asks the waiters – who run around rattled – what they think? In the kitchen extra care is taken with the supposed inspector's food.

If he orders a roasted pike-perch steak with a 'meat jus', the second will inspect the piece of fish, tweezers in hand, in search of a potential fishbone. The lemon slice will also have to be recut, its points deemed not sufficiently regular. The chef will check his medallions of filet mignon a hundred times to make sure they are cooked to perfection. He will give an apprentice hell for leaving a piece of skin on a broad bean. The maître d' comes to report back. He must describe the guest's expression when presented with his dish, say if he left anything or if he made any comments? Was he reminded that everything was, of course, cooked from scratch? That the restaurant is known for its nougat glacé, its raspberry coulis? No? He only had fruit salad? How odd for a gastronomic critic. 'Make sure to give him some macaroons with his dessert. I will walk around the restaurant and casually say hello,' he informs us. He changes his apron and shoes and makes his appearance in the restaurant. He chats with regulars, serves aperitifs to some guests waiting for their table, then makes his way towards the mystery guest, who is talking loudly with an awkward-looking maître d': 'Well done, chef, I was just telling your maître d' that I'll come back to your establishment when I next have a meeting with the mayor.' The Michelin man will not be making an appearance tonight. 'Another fail,' one apprentice whispers to another in the kitchen.

The chef and his second make us pay dearly on days like these. Long-forgotten is our afternoon break. There we will be, peeling and preparing a mountain of Jerusalem artichokes and spinach, skinning tomatoes and concocting bases and stocks. The second will find any excuse to give the apprentices hell, punching their arms and pulling their ears. The kids are exhausted and undernourished. The staff never get a proper meal. We eat what cannot be served in the restaurant, on the cusp of being edible. I am hungry. One evening I pick at a plate that has come back barely touched. The second loudly insults me, calling me a 'sponger'. I don't argue. Fatigue has wiped out my courage. I want to finish as quickly as possible because I need to get back to my books at home. But the service goes on for ever. Later on we must yet again listen to the chef lecturing the apprentices, who are dropping with exhaustion. He reminds them that 'it's a privilege to be fed and housed'. In reality they have nothing to eat, and they sleep with the rats under the roof. I saw one of them cry several times. One Monday morning he never returned. 'He wasn't cut out for this profession, anyway,' the chef said.

Though his second appears to be a bona-fide sadist, I still cannot decide for certain what to make of the boss. One morning, when I was struggling to prepare a rack of lamb, he came over with his boning knife and showed me how to remove the meat at the top of the ribs to leave them bare. He told me that, aged fourteen, he had worked in an abattoir in Vosges before becoming an apprentice in a kitchen. As I watched him scrape the bones clean to ensure they didn't colour during cooking, I understood his pathological obsession with perfection, trapping him in a life without a wife or children, where the only thing that mattered was the service. Other people were not important.

You are like him. Often I wondered if maybe Hélène left because she was fed up with always seeing you with your pots and pans. What with the phone box and the front door, it's no surprise that I have still not got in touch with her. I am frightened of hearing words that will flay you. And yet, I don't see her as someone who would blame you. It's facts that I want: they would be enough for me. I remember what Gaby said: 'Crazy about your dad as well.'

'When I am not in the kitchen I try not to lose sight of my lessons at the Rue Megevand. I come bursting into the lecture theatre, sometimes straight from the kitchen. 'Can you smell food?' my neighbour says to me. I smile, thinking about what Corinne used to say to me. I have completely given up trying to understand Corneille, but I am diligent in my comparative literature classes. Mr Bushy Hair with the big beak has understood that I am not the type to go to the parties that the law and medical students hold.

'What have you been doing with your hands?' he asked me one day when I'd burnt myself. I told him I had done it working on my motorbike, which was clearly not the case.

'What make?'

'It's Yamaha for me, the XT 500,' I lied, thinking back to my schooldays.

'I see, Japanese,' he persisted. 'Me, I'm more of an English man, Norton or a Triumph.'

When I'm not lying, I struggle to fill the silences. Three years of technical education have driven an unfathomable gulf between me and those taking literature. I love words, but they slip through my fingers like the fish that I would try and catch by hand with Gaby. When I don't know something or don't understand it, I pretend that I do. But sometimes the tightrope walker takes a tumble. I am doing a presentation on Shakespeare, feeling about as calm as I would be making a crème pâtissière in the pitch black. I talk at length about the 'fictional' and 'symbolic' death of a character, then come to my conclusion, relieved. Mr Beak has kept on his black cape. He looks like a crow perched in the middle of a tree. He turns towards my fellow students and asks: 'So, what do you think?'

Silence in the lecture theatre, a few voices murmur, 'Good.'

'Well, I have just one question,' he says. 'You talk about fictional and symbolic death. Why not just one of these epithets? What's the difference between the two, according to you?'

I mumble a few nonsensical sentences. Amused, he lets me dig myself ever deeper into a hole until, *in extremis*, he brings me back. 'Wouldn't it be more appropriate to talk about a fictional death, does that make sense to you?'

I say yes with the speed of someone who has just signed his jail-release form.

'All's well then, it was very good.'

I am not used to compliments. In the kitchen I am frequently told, 'We are cooking for the customers, not for fun.' I head back up the lecture theatre steps.

Mr Beak calls after me: 'You don't need to be so nervous. These are just words and paper. I don't doubt you're more relaxed in the kitchen.'

I have been publicly exposed.

'You can't hide anything here. Especially when you take the restaurant dustbins out.'

We climb the stairs together. Just before we get to the swinging doors, he turns to me: 'I have a lot of admiration for people who work with their hands.'

One evening I lend a hand to the apprentices so they can tidy up their stations more quickly. It's the end of the service. The chef has gone. The kitchen porter has just finished scrubbing the floor. He is a Kurd who has recently arrived in France. He is called Agrîn and has been recruited that morning. He is paid in cash, by the day. The second piles on the bullying with these illegal workers. One day it's a frying pan that he decides has not been properly cleaned; the next, the washing up is not being done quickly enough. Today the second is particularly vicious with the kitchen porter, who had balked at the second's demand to scour the same casserole pot twice. The second is now set on making him pay. He has deliberately poured the last of some gravy onto the clean floor tiles. Sniggering, he claims it was an accident, and orders Agrîn to wash the kitchen floor again. The porter quietly says 'no', one of the few words he knows in French. 'Do what I tell you, or you're sacked.' The second gets up, picks up the cloth from some greasy water in the sink, and throws it at the feet of the porter, who stands there impassive. 'Pick it up.' Agrîn folds his arms. 'Listen to me, you dirty Arab, clean your shit or I'll kick your arse.' A flicker of a smile, then the porter hurls what is evidently not a compliment in Kurdish. At this the second goes for him, I get in between them just in time. He crashes into me, surprised and now even more furious. 'You as well, eh, you're sticking up for this scum? Get out of my way so I can stick one on him.' Behind me Agrîn panics: 'No, no.'

'Stay out of this, smart arse.' The second has called me 'smart arse' ever since he saw me reading by the dustbins. He is head-butting the air in the direction of the porter, I push him back. He comes back at me, I do a kickbox move on him, he skids across the wet tiles, all the while shouting at me breathlessly that 'you're just a commis chef from a brothel. Like your father.' I hear Gaby in my head telling me, 'It's not necessarily the strongest who wins a fight, it's the meanest.' I take the cloth and stuff it in the second's mouth. He grabs my balls and twists them. The pain increases my violence. I grab a frying pan. I'm about to smash his face with it when I feel an iron grip holding me back. Agrîn is looking at me, his eyes surprisingly gentle.

'No,' he says, putting the pan back down on the cooker.

I am relieved to be fired.

5

One Sunday morning someone is knocking on the door of my room. I have a horrendous hangover. I've had too many beers with Agrîn and some activists – the last of the Mohicans – toasting the Kurdish Workers' Party and the Revolutionary Communist League at the university bar. I open the door to you, bare-chested and scratching my beard. You look at me hard, a bag of croissants in your hand. 'I have to get in my car to see you, do I?'

I yawn to cover up my embarrassment. 'Aren't you going to let me in?' You are the first to visit my little roost. I awkwardly fold my bed cover and invite you to sit on my one and only chair.

'Do you have coffee?'

I point to the jar of instant coffee by my toothbrush, and run some hot water from the tap. I can tell you're disappointed by my basic set-up. 'You should have told me, I would have brought you an electric coffee-maker.'

I only have one mug for us both. We share it, dipping the croissants into the coffee. You inspect every little corner of the room, lingering on the piles of books that clutter my desk, the notes tacked onto the wallpaper.

'Why didn't you say anything? I would have given you some more money.'

'What for?'

'To get yourself a bigger place.'

'It's not about size, I'm happy here.'

'What do you do to eat?'

'I manage, I'm not that hungry.'

You don't seem very convinced. I proudly open my old tobacco tin where I keep my savings. 'Look, I've got enough to be going on with.'

'Hang on, you're not spending anything I send you each month?'

'I earn a bit doing little jobs.'

I could not have hurt you any more if I had sunk a knife through your heart.

'So, this cooking thing is still going on, is it?'

'It's not a "thing". It's my life.' I add: 'Just like the books are.'

You put your head in your hands. 'Jesus, how did this damn bug get into your system?'

'It was just down to me, watching you do your job.'

'I have already told you: it's not a proper job.'

You point at the books. 'And all this, what's it for?'

'To discover the world. I know the opportunity you're giving me by letting me study.'

'Then study. Don't waste your time over plates of food – become a teacher.'

'I am not wasting my time. I want to be able to read, write and cook.'

You massage your temples, your head down. 'Then come and help me over the summer holidays.'

'Sure, but that's not enough, Dad. I want to experience other things. Like I said before, I want to study and cook.'

'Dammit! At your age I had to go and graft in a bakery because I could barely write my name.'

'Exactly. I want you to be proud of your profession through me.'

'What? Being bored shitless fifteen hours a day for idiots who come to you to eat and shit. You call that a profession, do you?'

'Maybe, if you'd given more time to Hélène, if she was still with us, you'd see things differently.'

I have just hit the nuclear war button. I am aware of this but feel as though I don't have much left to lose. For so long this misunderstanding has lived between us. You stand up from the chair and grab me by the collar. I think you are going to hit me. You shake me violently.

'Don't ever talk to me about that woman. Do you hear me? Not ever again.'

You can't even say Hélène's name. If she knew, living just a few hundred metres away, what a state you've got into just by hearing her name . . . I look at you; you are bright red, dressed in your awful Sunday best, a jacquard pullover, your trousers rumpled over your shoes, sitting on my handkerchief on the bed. Hélène is probably eating breakfast while marking exercise books in her town mansion, or preening in front of a mirror before she gets into her German car.

The rain begins to pound on the fanlight. You light a Gitane. You cannot bear an impasse. 'Well then, what do we do?

'I do my two-year general literature degree and work in restaurants on the side.'

You pull furiously on your cigarette. 'Then I'm stopping your allowance.'

It's final. You slam the door of my room; the Led Zeppelin poster falls to the ground. You have forgotten your cigarettes. I light one and go back to bed. You are indeed the unbelievably 'stubborn mule' that Gaby once described to me. A pit of sadness opens up in me.

6

I find employment with Amar. He has taken over a little restaurant at the top of the Rue Battant and is looking for someone to help him. We get to know each other standing over the cooker in his tiny kitchen, where Agrîn quickly takes up residence as kitchen porter. Amar had handed me a commis apron even before I had begun to work for him. 'Have you heard of *mulukhiyah*?' Needless to say, I haven't. 'It's a celebratory dish, like for the first day of spring.' He showed me some soft green powder: 'It's the powder of the jute mallow, a plant that grows at the base of palm trees. We use it in the sauce.' After caressing a long skewer of deep red chuck steak, he cuts himself a piece. 'It's beautiful, isn't it?' Someone who appreciated chuck steak like my father had taught me to do could never be a bad man in my books. He had coated the meat with garlic and a beautiful sienna-coloured powder. 'This is besar, a mix of spices made by my mother. She uses cinnamon, caraway and fennel,' Amar had said to me as he added some Espelette pepper, olive oil and tomato purée to concoct a pungent-smelling paste for the chuck steak.

Amar told me about his childhood spent on the other side of Mediterranean. His mother washed the spices in a palm sieve and cooked *mulukhiyah*. 'Today I repeat every one of her movements.

Throughout my whole childhood I watched her cook. I would go shopping for her, buy the fish at the port, take the turmeric to be ground at the local miller's.' His father had left their village backwater to work in a foundry in France. I thought back to the little soldiers of Taylorism, the 'Maghrebis' looked down upon by my high-school teacher.

'When he left to travel to France to work, my father told me: 'You are the father of your brothers now, you can't go misbehaving in the streets.' Whenever his father wrote it was Amar who read the letters out to his mother. The son imagined his father's life by following the stages of the Tour de France, discovering each of the regions and their produce. To this day Amar is unbeatable on the geography and cheeses of France. He worked every sort of job before crossing the Mediterranean and stepping off a train at the Gare de Viotte in Besançon one morning at dawn.

Amar poured the jute mallow powder into some warm olive oil, where it turned a bottle-green colour. He then added the pieces of chuck steak, which he had simmered in a perfumed mix of chopped herbs and mushrooms.

I have opened the door into a world that fascinates me, the world of spices. At my father's place all I ever knew was pepper, allspice and nutmeg. Through Amar I learn about the cardamom he puts in his rice pudding, the turmeric he adds to his meatballs, the cinnamon for his citrus syrup and the star anise for veal kidney. Before telling me all about his first steps in cooking, he was insistent I should try his *chorba* with cuttlefish. 'It will melt in your mouth, but it still needs some more garlic and celery.'

He had started off as a kitchen porter, after which an old chef took him under his wing. He learnt a culinary mix of bourgeois home cooking and bistro dishes, where a simple rabbit in mustard sat side by side next to *sole meunière* and *crêpes suzette*. When his mentor retired, Amar found himself head of a kitchen.

The *mulukhiyah* was cooked, glistening like a pool of black ink. Amar decorated his piece of chuck steak with three bay leaves. Now the colour of cocoa, the meat melted in the mouth and the sauce was as silky as a ganache truffle, with a delicate green flavour. We ate it simply with bread.

With Amar I learnt that cooking could be the meeting point of many different approaches. He cooked Morteau sausage in a cassoulet using his mother's spices; he taught me to how to prepare couscous grains to accompany a *boeuf bourguignon*; he showed me his recipe for a *duck à l'orange pastilla*.

When I tie my commis chef's apron on, I never know whether I will get an object lesson in his orange-flower water, or his version of *patates en cocotte*, which could have come straight out of a Vosges kitchen but for the turmeric he uses to enliven it. For him spice isn't there as the 'icing on the cake'; it's telling the story of the men who live between the Rue Battant and the other side of the Mediterranean. Amar laughs at those who still don't understand. 'When I'm at home in my village backwater, they say, "Make pizza", and when I'm here, they say, "Make couscous."' Agrîn describes him as like the fig tree: he grows upwards but never turns his back on his tentacle-like roots.

On Sundays, Amar's little restaurant turns into a rowdy inn where regulars and passers-by meet for a long, drawn-out coffees, a glass of Chardonnay or the traditional snack enjoyed around Lyon, *mâchon*. People read the *Est Républicain*, relive the FC–Sochaux match, or indulge in some gentle flirting in the hope of a delicious afternoon in bed. Amar is a bit like the travelling minstrel of the Rue Battant. He leaves me to it in the kitchen with Agîr.

We can give free rein to our inspiration. Each Sunday I do

exactly that with my magnum opus, a potato omelette done with spring onions, coriander, and whatever chilli I find in the pantry. Agîr makes his famous aubergine dip and cucumbers in yoghurt. I also make dolmades with him, those vine leaves stuffed with rice that you will grow to like so much when you become ill.

On this morning I launch into the creation of a pilaf that I will serve on a huge plate on the table for diners. Up until now I can't deny that rice has always seemed like hard-going stodge for me, but necessary with a *blanquette de veau* or Friday fish. We had epic-length discussions, you and me, on how to cook pasta, rice and vegetables. You came from that era when they were cooked on a roaring hot stove, even if that meant serving them as soggy as mush. When I started to cook green beans al dente, you asked me if I was planning to go out of business. You went on and on about it: 'This is all just a fashion.' Your curiosity got the better of you in the end, though. I remember the fuss you made when you first tried my pilaf rice: 'It's not cooked.' Later, you would ask me, 'Will you do some of your rice?'

I like the rice when it starts to hiss in the butter of the pan. It turns golden, releasing a scent of toasted hazelnuts. I like it when the ladles of stock make the rice vibrate before it begins to bubble gently and absorb the liquid. I am in the middle of browning some pine nuts and raisins to add to the rice when Amar calls to me: 'Somebody's here for you.'

I recognise Gaby's imposing silhouette. He is wearing an English camouflage jacket which clearly intrigues the other clients. He has let his hair and white beard grow. He winks as he comes towards me, a punnet in hand: 'Here, put this away. Home delivery. It's wild asparagus straight to you from my neck of the woods. And keep it quiet here about where it's come from.'

I offer him a coffee while Gaby rolls a cigarette. He cheerfully ignores any kind of rules, not least about smoking in a bistro. He doesn't seem to be in a hurry. 'Are you going to stay and eat with us?'

He hesitates. 'OK, but quickly, as I didn't tell Maria where I was.'

I pan-fry a large handful of the asparagus, to which I add the rice. I make us a large plate.

'Don't you want to eat outside? It's nice out,' Gaby suggests.

We go and sit on a bench in the square, opposite the restaurant. Gaby toys with his spoon as I tuck in. I don't believe for a moment that he is here to share the proceeds of his pilfering. He looks at me, his eyes serious: 'Your father is sick.'

Gaby has never skimped on words, especially when he's messing about, but his sentences become short when he needs to get to the point. He doesn't wait for my response.

'Lung cancer. They can remove some of it but he doesn't want that.' He chews his mouthful for a long time.

'How long have you known?'

He looks bothered. 'It's been a little while. He didn't want anyone to tell you.'

'And why doesn't he want surgery?'

'He says he doesn't want to feel diminished, and that he's screwed anyway, everything is screwed now.'

'Sounds like him. He's always known best.'

'He doesn't believe in the docs when they tell him that he has a good chance of pulling through. Also, the restaurant, it's not doing very well.'

'What do you mean?'

'Your father has started showing his age. My brother can't do everything. I think he's also been undercut by the competition.

People prefer going to the shopping centre for lunch, eating in cafeterias, you know?'

'Does he talk about me?'

'He says that you've gone off now to live your life. That with your studies, you'll be set.'

'And my cooking? Will he still not hear a word about it?'

Gaby sighs. He puts down his spoon and puts his hand on my shoulder. 'You'd best go and see him, kid. You need to talk.'

'You think that's easy, do you?'

'Don't make the same stupid mistakes we did. Our fathers were ravaged by the war of 1914. They came back crippled, drunk, mute. Talk to each other, for Christ's sake.'

'Who knows about his cancer?'

'Me, Maria, Lucien, Nicole.'

'So, the family basically. And Hélène?'

Gabriel frowns as if I've just said a massively incongruous thing. 'Hélène?'

'Well yeah, Hélène. She shared his life, my life.'

'But no one knows where she is.'

'I do.'

I get the impression that our conversation is making Gaby's head spin, particularly when I add: 'I will talk to her.'

I accompany Gaby back to his 4L, rolling myself a cigarette with his tobacco, the Scaferlati.

'You're going to go and see him?'

'Once I've seen Hélène.'

Everything goes quickly, like the films in my childhood when you could speed up images by turning the projector handle faster. I drink a cup of boukha tea then dial Hélène's number. A man's voice answers.

'Sorry to bother you. May I talk to Hélène?'

'She's here. I'll pass you over.'

'Hello?'

'Hello, this is Julien.'

I hear children's voices. Hélène says: 'Could you close the door, please?'

7

I am sitting on the banks of the Doubs. I am skimming stones on the river to stave off boredom. A magical act. She will arrive when the stone has bounced three times. My hands are shaking. In the end it was the trainers I saw first, when I had been expecting tall boots. She is wearing faded jeans and a fisherman's jumper. Her hair is pulled back in a ponytail. Her skin seems darker than in my memory. I stand up and walk up the slope of the bank. I recognise her perfume when she kisses me hello. She is trying to smile, in spite of her emotion. I don't know what to say, except, rather awkwardly, 'Where shall we go?' She says; 'A walk, would that be OK?' It would be.

The grass is covered with daffodils. I keep my eyes on them, extremely troubled. I know that she knows. She wisely sticks to asking me about my studies. We talk about Goldoni, who enter-tains me, Robbe-Grillet, who intrigues me and Gracq, whose books – published by Corti – I like a lot. She looks amused.

'Your comparative literature professor likes you a lot.'

'How do you know?'

'He's a friend.'

'How on earth did you know I was in his class?'

I can hear the sound of water flowing against a stone dam;

willow buds float through the air. She looks at me tenderly. When her words come they are so obviously full of affection. Just like when Mr Beak the beanpole explains all of life to us in Shakespeare.

'You never left me, Julien, all these years. Even when I got married and had children. You were always with me. And it's a small world. I kept in touch with some of your teachers at school and high school. They kept me informed about your life.'

'And your phone number, how did you get it to me?'

'Through your French teacher. She felt you were going to go on and study literature.'

I feel the anger rising. 'So, you secretly spied on me while we were left in the shit?'

'That's not how it was.'

'It was you who left, right?'

I am hunched over, rolling a cigarette, but I can sense her embarrassed silence.

'Would you roll me one, please?'

'They're strong.'

'As strong as your father's Gitanes?'

'He has lung cancer. That's what made me decide to see you. He is refusing treatment.'

Hélène turned her head abruptly towards the Doubs river. She takes a long puff of the cigarette, then says in a low, still voice: 'It wasn't love at first sight when I met your father. It was when I saw him on his own with you that I fell in love with him. Very much. I was from a different background, but I immediately felt comfortable with you both. I loved your father for who he was. I loved his hands ruined from cooking. I have never loved a man's hands more than your father's. I loved his worker's wisdom but also his lack of knowledge. His questions would touch me when I was talking about a book or an author. When he didn't know something he wouldn't pretend like other people did.'

'Then why on earth did you leave?'

Hélène stares at me, pain in her eyes. 'I wanted us to get married. It wasn't much to ask. It wasn't so much the marriage that was important to me but being able to adopt you. Your father didn't want to. I didn't push it too hard because I didn't want to make your father feel rushed. He was still caught up in grief about your mum. When you first started calling me Mum, it made me happy but it was also painful. One day he said to me: "You have brought the light back into my life." But I don't think he could ever escape the darkness.'

'Because of my mother?'

'Undoubtedly, but it wasn't just that. He loved me very deeply, but he was haunted by things, shadows from long ago. His childhood in the Morvan, Algeria . . . even if he never talked about it.'

'Why didn't you have a child together?'

'He didn't want to have any more. There was only you for him.'

'In the way of everyone's happiness, basically.'

'Never say that. He loves you more than anything.'

'Yes, but badly.'

'We love how we can. Being a parent is the hardest job of all.'

Hélène walks off into the night through the trees of the Parc Chamars. Before she leaves she kisses me and says quietly: 'If only you knew how much I missed you.'

8

It's a Sunday in autumn. We are by the river. You are sitting propped against a tree. I have placed a cushion behind your back and a blanket down on the grass. You don't complain. Your body is swarming with metastasis. The doctors can only dispense what they call 'supportive care'. You are munching crisps with a glass of Côtes du Rhône. I have bought a roast chicken.

'Dad, which bit do you want?'

'As if you don't know!'

'The wings and the parson's nose?'

'One wing will do.'

I was about to say 'you must eat' but it would have been foolish. The chicken is dry and flavourless.

'We've known better chicken, haven't we?'

You gnaw at your wing. You tidy away the bones in a bag and take a pear. You peel and cut it up with your Pradel knife. 'You want a quarter?'

'Yes, please.'

'It's a fine fruit, the pear. It will see you through the winter.'

You stare beyond the river and add: 'When you're in your kitchen.'

I swallow a large gulp of wine that drowns my heart. I am

incapable of replying. Emotion has rendered me speechless. You know this, even if you are not looking at me. You are wading through the silence. 'There's a coypu over there, swimming along the riverbank. You know that coypu is delicious in a ragout or terrine, don't you?'

You are talking to me about coypu while shaking my life like a plum tree. 'Can you throw this carcass in the water for me – it'll make the fishes happy.'

I obey you like a child.

'And when you do a chicken, always in a casserole dish in the oven. With a lemon in its arse. The important thing is to baste it regularly with the juices.'

You bite a piece of pear, shrugging your shoulders. 'Well, I don't even know why I am telling you all this. You watched me do all of it, didn't you?'

I leap upright. I am filled with tears and fury. I want to shout, 'And what about me? What am I going to do when you're no longer here?' I see your death as it nears, your absence, the noise of your pots and pans at seven in the morning, a sound which will never be the same. Coffee without you. Peeling vegetables without you. Onions turning golden in the casserole pot without you. Terrine without you. The smell of burning without you yelling at me: 'Careful with your potatoes, they're getting caught!' There will be no final morsel of brawn to share before your last Gitanes of the day.

I am striding along the riverbank. A strange, wordless joy overcomes my anger. You have just passed the baton to me, between the parson's nose of a dodgy chicken and a pack of ready-made crisps. You are handing over. As simply as if you had asked me for 'the salt' or to 'turn the crêpe over'. I find this ambush almost cruel. But it's you, and you have seen the cook in me. You are standing up. You are by the riverbank. You turn me around. 'Sit down, kiddo.'

The worst thing is that I do as you say, like a little kid.

'Do you remember your *Tout Univers* books?'

'Yes.'

'Your head was constantly buried in those books; it gave me such pleasure buying them for you. I was so proud of how much you knew.'

Silence.

'Now I'm the one reading them. I can't stop. I can never get enough of their pages. The truth is I had to get into this state to start learning. That's why I wanted you to go to school.'

'But Dad, you have hands of gold.'

'Poor man's gold. When you're plating a dish, no one sees you. When you're in the shit in the kitchen, no one hears you. People, they eat. That's it.'

'People come to the Relais Fleuri because of what you do.'

'For what I did, Julien.'

'No, not true. People still come for your veal's head, your bourguignon. Everyone knows you *are* the Relais Fleuri. If you'd wanted it, we could have got a star.'

You smile at me. 'There are no great chefs, just great restaurants. The Relais Fleuri? It's just a little boozer opposite a train station.'

'The Troisgros brothers have their three stars. Each of you has a cult dish: they've got their salmon fillet with sorrel, you your vol-au-vents.'

You burst out laughing. 'You never doubt yourself, do you?'

'And do you begrudge me that?'

'God, no. I was the one who doubted your ability to study at university and learn this godforsaken craft.'

'And now?'

'You have your kitchen and your books. Only you can know your future. What you have learnt can never be lost.'

I turn on the cooker to heat some water. I measure out the coffee with your ladle. Lulu's moped is purring in the courtyard. I look at the clock: 7.30. I am peeling carrots and onions to make the stock for veal sweetbreads in vermouth. You are my hands when I place the sweetbreads in butter, my eyes when I watch them turn brown, and my intuition when I add the vermouth and stock a little at a time. Lucien is surprised when I ask him to taste it.

'A little bit more pepper,' he suggests.

'Why doesn't my dad taste things any more when he cooks?'

'I think he lost his sense of taste.'

'What?'

'He never really explained it to me. It was after your mother died, and especially after Hélène left. I could see it was a problem, he was never comfortable.'

'How did he manage?'

Lulu bites his lip, as if worried he'll say the wrong thing. 'You know him, he always went by the crook in his hand to judge salt. Everything else, he just did it off the top of his head. And then at times, between dishes, he would go: "Did you taste it, Lulu?"'

'And did you taste it?'

'Yeah, no, I'd pretend. He never gets it wrong.'

Each evening, at 6.30, I take up two bowls of soup that we eat together. You particularly like a potato and watercress one. You tell me about the book, *Les Colonnes du ciel* by Bernard Clavel, which I devoured as an adolescent and you are in the middle of reading. You are fascinated by how a writer can place the action of his book in familiar settings. You tell me about La Vieille-Loye, a village in the middle of the Forest of Chaux, where you went mushroom-picking and fished for minnows.

I may well have put an armchair for you in the kitchen, but you never come to sit on it. You prefer sitting in the courtyard outside. You need air. As for cooking, you never talk about it any more, to me or Lucien. One day I pick up a couple of nice chickens at the market. My idea is to do them the Gaston Gérard way, but I want to ask you for your version of the Dijon recipe that combines Comté cheese and mustard. You don't even look up from your book. 'I'm sure what you do will be very good.' You prefer to discuss *Le Seigneur du fleuve* with me. Bernard Clavel again. I stand there at a loss. Even the novelties I put on your plate don't elicit a raised eyebrow from you. I have put mackerel fillets with a soy and ginger sauce on the menu, along with the pilau rice I've learnt to make from Amar. I am not sure about this move because the regulars don't come to the Relais Fleuri in search of the exotic. Lucien looks thoughtful when he sees me coming back with a box full of spices, or when I flavour the oil with cumin, star anise and fennel seeds. You taste the mackerel, examine the grains of rice with your fork. I watch you from my cooker. When you bring back your plate you have a little smile on your face. You had a dish of chocolate mousse instead of your Gitanes. You blithely study my meals on your plate but don't say a word. You go back to your books and documentaries on TV.

I think back to the questions you used to ask Hélène when she was marking schoolwork or preparing her lessons. You can finally quench your thirst for knowledge. I don't know if you have turned into someone else, or if I finally know you. Your actions and advice come alive to me when I use your 'tools', as you say. At first I was awkward. My palm and fingers would fiddle with the handle and blades that had only ever known your hand. When I am struggling, Lulu never says to me: 'Your father would have done it like this,' just, 'You should hold it this way.'

In the evening, after the service, I gently push open your door. You tell me to turn on the bedside lamp. You ask me why I don't become a cook for a Russian billionaire. 'You could earn millions. You could turn the Relais Fleuri into a Relais & Chateau.' We have a good laugh about that. I know that, deep down, you fear the moment I go to sleep on the bed that you slept on, near your ovens. As the nights go by I stay with you more and more. You are like those children who are scared to be alone in the dark, who cling when it's time to sleep. Sometimes the morphine takes you on solitary journeys, you gasp through painful dreams. But when I come back the next day and you have the strength, you still want me to take you for a little walk.

I get you into the car, play Michel Delpech on the radio, and we go walking down the towpath by the canal. You show me a pile of ruins overgrown with creepers and bramble. You tell me how it was an open-air café and dance hall where you would come to eat deep-fried gudgeon and dance with my mother. A little before Christmas you want to go to the cemetery. We go by the florist's. I get white roses. When I come back to the car, you whisper: 'Not those ones. I told you, the Christmas roses.' I go back to buy hellebore flowers. You contemplate them. As if you are thinking about how they will decorate you both together, with Mum. Soon.

Epilogue

'You have the same hands as him.'

'Why do you say that?'

'The brown marks on your hands and the red palms.'

'They're burns – heat marks from the cooker and casseroles.'

'I know.'

I am beating an omelette. Hélène takes me by the hand. I let the fork fall into the egg.

'Close your eyes.'

'Why?'

'Just listen to me, don't be scared.'

I feel her hand guide mine towards the worktop. 'Look.'

I recognise the leather cover. It's the recipe book. I turn around as if you're right there behind me. Hélène smiles.

'He wanted me to bring it to you after it was all over. I called him after I saw you again. We spoke for a long time.'

I hesitate before touching the book. In truth it never left me. By taking it away from me you increased my desire to learn this profession you found so hard to pass on. I start beating the omelette again.

'How did he give it to you?'

'Is that important for you?'

'Yes.' I stop beating the omelette: 'Actually, deep down, no, not really.'

I had often imagined myself finding your recipe book, the joy at seeing it. Today I am peaceful as I roll the omelette around the pan. I ended up opening it at the first recipes copied down by Hélène. Then the writing, still in pencil, changed, and carried on to the last page. You have written down all of your recipes, from quenelles with a gratin, to a *navarin* of lamb, by way of raspberry jam. Each is underlined. Ingredients are carefully indicated. As is the cooking time. You have even gone so far as to make little comments: 'When choosing cardoons, the preference is for small ones, matte-white in colour.'

On each page there is something of you. From your first Gitanes in the morning while drinking your jug of coffee; your silent moods that only Lucien could decipher; your generosity that ensured you never became rich; your humility in always taking a back seat to your dishes; your talent at holding the service together when everyone wanted their food at once or a dish needed adjusting; that invisible imagination that inspired you to make a dish out of practically nothing; your respect for every ingredient from a breadcrumb to a mushroom; the stubbornness that kept you cooking your life away from 7 a.m. till 11 p.m. without a word of complaint.

'Did he give you his pencil?'

'Yes, have it.'

I feel the worn-down pencil between my fingers. On the first page, still blank, I write:

Good cooking is all in the memory – Georges Simenon.

Jacky Durand on setting his novel in Eastern France:

I've set my novel in Eastern France, a region that doesn't share the celebrity of wine-renowned Burgundy, or the late Paul Bocuse's Lyon. It's a somewhat plain region, but it's this plainness that gives French cuisine its singularity: delighting you in turn with a simple homemade boeuf bourguignon or a veal chop elevated to the sublime in the hands of chef Pierre Gagnaire. The ordinary and the extraordinary go hand in hand as far as the pleasure of the taste buds is concerned.

I wanted to evoke a France that is always at the dining table, eating. Sharing the pleasure of a meal, be it the most simple of dishes, or Michelin-starred fine cuisine. Swapping memories of meals eaten, too, remembering flavours from childhood, passing recipes on to the next generation. France remains, today, and hopefully tomorrow, a country where we eat while talking about what we have eaten before and are yet to eat. Chatting about the *blanquette de veau* as Grandma used to make it, as well as the salmon in sorrel sauce that made the fame of the Troisgros brothers in Roanne.

The Little French Recipe Book tells all of this, through the story of a small bistro opposite a rural train station. With the wish to pay tribute to all the women and men who, every day, bring us so much joy from the anonymity of their kitchens. You could almost say, there are no great or humble chefs. There is just the generosity of showing love through food. The taste of life, if you will.

Recipe

The Little Soup of Happiness

Two carrots
One leek
A little knob of butter
A cube of chicken stock

Peel the carrots; trim and wash the leek. You will use only the white: the green, minced and braised in a pan with a bit of butter, will go marvellously with a piece of fish. For our soup, chop the carrots and the white of the leek into a *julienne* of small di.

In a small saucepan, fry the vegetables with the butter. Wet it then with half a litre of water (or more if you like a clearer soup), add your stock cube and a few grinds of black pepper, cover it, then – *hop!* – leave your masterpiece to hum under the lid for a few minutes, until the vegetables melt in the mouth.

Serve preferably in a glass bowl, for this julienne is as pleasing on the eye as it is on the taste buds. Of course, you can mop it all up with some stale bread, add a handful of vermicelli, or a tablespoon of crème fraîche

Dandelion Salad

One tablespoon of mustard
One tablespoon of red wine vinegar
600g dandelion leaves
200g bacon
One tablespoon of olive oil
Black pepper

In a bowl, whisk the mustard and vinegar together with the pepper. Add the dandelion leaves, which you have washed and dried. Cut the bacon into lardons and fry until golden in a pan with the oil. Pour them, and the oil they have released during cooking, over the dandelion leaves, stir in and serve.

You can add to this salad some walnuts, boiled eggs, or croutons rubbed with garlic.

Gratin, Comtois-style

A kilo of potatoes
Two garlic cloves
A good piece of Comté
200g of bacon
Butter
Ground pepper
A glass of dry white wine (optional)

Peel and slice a good kilo of potatoes (preferably Charlotte or Roseval). Mince the garlic cloves, grate the cheese and chop the bacon into lardons. Generously butter a dish and add a layer of potatoes, followed by a sprinkling of salt. Then layer a handful of lardons, grated cheese, a little garlic, a few slivers of butter and some ground pepper, then repeat until you finish with a top layer of cheese. You can also moisten with a glass of dry white wine. Put in the oven for forty-five minutes at 220°C.

Serve with a fresh seasonal salad.

Boeuf–Carottes

A kilo of carrots
Butter
Peanut oil
A kilo of beef chuck cut into large chunks
Four shallots, peeled and finely chopped
Three celery leaves
One bay leaf
One sprig of thyme
Salt and pepper

Clean the carrots and peel them. Chop them into chunky dice. In a large cooking pot, melt two knobs of butter with a trickle of oil, and seal each side of the chunks of meat. Add the shallots. When they have taken on a golden colour, add the carrots and the celery leaves. Season with the salt and pepper, and add the bay leaf and thyme. Cover and leave to simmer for at least three hours.

It may be necessary to add a little hot water while the meat cooks, as it must be perfectly tender. Depending on your tastebuds, you might want to add some cumin, orange zest, preserved lemon, ras el-hanout, fresh coriander, tarragon, black olives . . .

Serve on its own, or with some pasta, rice or potatoes.

Pot-au-Feu

An oxtail cut into pieces, tied with string
A kilo of short rib
A kilo of beef chuck
Six marrow bones
An onion studded with two cloves
A bouquet garni of parsley, thyme, two bay leaves and a celery
stalk tied together
Four turnips
Four carrots
Three leeks
Six potatoes, parboiled for a few minutes
Five black peppercorns
Sea salt

Add all the meat to a cooking pot with the onion, the bouquet garni, the salt and the peppercorns. Cover everything with cold water. Bring to the boil. With a sieve, regularly skim the debris which will form at the surface. Cook gently for two and a half to three hours. During that time, peel and wash your vegetables. Trim half of the leek, saving the stalk. Add the vegetables to the meat, and allow a generous half-hour extra cooking time. Heat a serving plate in the oven, and then add the meat, surrounded by the vegetables and marrow bones.

Serve with cornichons, sea salt and wholegrain and Dijon mustards.

Monsieur Henri's Roast Chicken

One handsome free-range chicken
Butter
Four shallots
Two garlic cloves
A glass of water
A glass of white wine
20cl crème fraîche
One egg yolk
Salt and pepper

Carve the chicken into eight pieces. Season them with salt and pepper. Heat a nice knob of butter in a pan. Fry the chicken pieces, and when they have coloured, add the shallots and peeled garlic cloves and fry for a few minutes until golden. Add the water and the wine to the pan, cover and leave to simmer for twenty-five to thirty minutes. Remove the chicken pieces. In a bowl, carefully combine the crème fraîche and the egg yolk. Pour into the pan, and whisk with the cooking juices over a gentle heat. Then, add the chicken pieces back in, and cook for another three to four minutes.

Serve the chicken pieces with the sauce and some rice.

Jacky Durand

Stuffed Cabbage

A vegetable stock cube
One Savoy cabbage
Four shallots
Two garlic cloves
A few springs of flat leaf parsley
500g beef mince
500g sausagemeat
Two eggs
A kilo of very small potatoes
Salt, pepper, olive oil and your favourite seasonings: herbes de
Provence, Espelette chilli powder, pink peppercorns . . .

Heat a pan of water in which you have crumbled your stock cube. Whilst you bring it to the boil, gently separate the cabbage leaves and trim them. Once the water is boiling, blanch them for two to four minutes, until tender. Leave to drain. Peel the shallots and the garlic and mince finely. Chop the parsley. Mix in with the meat, the two eggs and season to taste. One by one, lay the cabbage leaves out on a chopping board, and spoon over a little of the stuffing mixture. Fold down the cabbage edges and roll tightly. Once you've stuffed all of them – you should have some cabbage leaves left – place on a baking tray, and drizzle with oil. You can add some salt, a few grinds of pepper and some pink peppercorns. Bake in the oven at 180°C.

Cover a separate baking tray with some of the remaining cabbage leaves, saving a few. Add the potatoes over the top, season, drizzle with olive oil and sprinkle some herbes de Provence or a sprig

166

of rosemary. Cover with the last cabbage leaves left, and bake until the potatoes are cooked, around forty minutes. Warm the stuffed cabbage leaves and serve together.

Mackerel in White Wine

A kilo small whole mackerel
Two onions
Two carrots
A bottle of Muscadet wine
Two thyme sprigs
A bay leaf
A clove
A few coriander seeds
20cl cider vinegar
A lemon
A few peppercorns
Salt

Gut and rinse the mackerel and carefully pat them dry. Place in a dish, powder with salt and leave them to rest for two hours. Meanwhile, peel and dice the onions and carrots. Place in a frying pan or casserole dish with the white wine and all the other ingredients bar the fish, vinegar and lemon. Boil for ten minutes, then add the vinegar and lemon, and cook for another five to ten minutes. Pat the mackerel down, then poach them in the stock for ten minutes. Then place them top-and-tail in a terrine and pour the stock over them.

Leave to refrigerate overnight and serve cold the next day.

Damson Tart

250g flour
100g butter
A pinch of salt
Half a cup of water
125g sugar
50g semolina flour
A kilo of damson plums
An egg yolk

First, sieve the flour into a large mixing bowl and add the butter in chunks, working it into the flour with the tips of your fingers. Combine the egg yolk with the salt and water and add to the mixture. Knead the dough for a minute or so – not longer as it will melt the butter! – and roll into a ball. Dust with flour, cover in clingfilm and refrigerate for an hour. Cover the bottom of a tart tin with baking paper, then line with the rolled-out pastry dough. Prick with a fork and then sprinkle over 50g sugar and 50g semolina flour which will absorb the juice from the damsons. Preheat your oven to 200°C.

Wash and pat dry a kilo of damsons. Chop in half and remove the stones. Carefully place the damsons over the pastry, face-up, forming a tight spiral. Sprinkle 75g sugar over the fruit and bake until the fruit caramelises.

Cherry Clafoutis

500g cherries, stalks removed
3 eggs
60g caster sugar, plus extra for topping
180g flour
50cl milk
Butter
Salt

Preheat your oven to 200°C. Wash and dry the cherries. Whisk together the eggs with the sugar and a pinch of salt. Slowly add the flour and then the milk, so that you have a smooth batter. If you want a slightly richer filling, you can also add 25g melted butter. Add the whole cherries (with stones!) to the mixture. Lightly grease a shallow baking dish and pour in the batter. Bake for between 45 minutes and an hour, until the top is golden, and the cherries are fragrant. Sprinkle with sugar as soon as it comes out of the oven. If it looks a little dry, you can also top with a couple of knobs of butter. This dessert can also be made with apricots or small plums.